Lock Down Publications and Ca$h
Presents

I0680373

THE BUTTERFLY MAFIA 2

The Stars Are Ours

Written By

FUMIYA PAYNE

First Edition 2023

Printed in the United States of America

This is a work of fiction. Names, characters, places, and incidents either are products of the author's imagination or are used fictitiously. Any similarity to actual events or locales or persons, living or dead, is entirely coincidental.

Lock Down Publications
P.O. Box 944
Stockbridge, GA 30281
www.lockdownpublications.com

Like our page on Facebook: Lock Down Publications
www.facebook.com/lockdownpublications.ldp

Stay Connected with Us!

Text **LOCKDOWN** to 22828 to stay up-to-date with new releases, sneak peaks, contests and more…

Like our page on Facebook:
Lock Down Publications

Join Lock Down Publications/The New Era Reading Group

Visit our website:
www.lockdownpublications.com

Follow us on Instagram:
Lock Down Publications

Email Us: We want to hear from you!

Acknowledgments

As usual, all praise to the Most High. Thank you for allowing my journey to continue, while so many others I know are no longer here. And though I love You to death, I'm in no hurry to meet you.(Lol)

Ca$h... I witnessed you walk from a prison cell to a production set. And If success was something easily attained, the whole world would own it. So I gotta send you a sincere salute, as your heard-earned achievements are admirable and inspiring.

Shawna P... Literally speaking, I think about you every single day of the year. Your absence has shown me the true value of your friendship. And at times I can't help but wonder if I lost you because I took you for granted, and had to be taught a lesson on the importance of appreciation. But damn, am I supposed to feel this lost and alone? You was the only person who ever believed in me, and now you're gone. But you know I'ma survivor by nature. So as much as I'll miss you until we link back up, I'ma continue to march through the rain and smile through the pain. Fumiya forever!

To my readers... Thank you for giving me a chance. And because I come straight from my heart, I hope that a character, a sentence, or something, will touch you on a level beyond just entertainment. And if I let you down in any way with this story, I promise to keep writing and pray I get better. So whatever you do, please don't give up on me.(and be sure to read my original poems at the end of each book)

Chapter 1

Bolting upright in bed, Asha awakened from her sleep as if she'd been doused with ice water. With her eardrums on the brink of bursting from the incessant pounding of her heart, she looked around in confusion before remembering she was at an Airbnb in Malibu, California.

Despite knowing Noni being endangered was just a dream, she still reached for her phone. And when her sister answered the Facetime call with a sleepy expression, Asha worriedly went in on her. "Why didn't you text me back, yesterday? I know you read them texts. Don't play with me, Noni. I'm telling you right now, girl."

Noni frowned. "Damn, yo, why you coming at me like that? It's four in the morning. And if you so worried, then you should've took me with you. So don't take your guilty conscious out on me."

"Girl, you know this was a business trip. We ain't come out here to kick it. So stop acting like a fucking baby!"

"I ain't acting like no baby. And you ain't gotta be cussing at me either."

Asha lowered the phone and took a moment to regain control of her emotions. It was just that the dream had felt so real. And even though they led unlawful lifestyles, she couldn't picture life without her sister's presence.

Bringing her face back into view, Asha inquired in a calm tone, "What you do yesterday?

"What you mean?" Noni dumbly replied.

"Just what I asked, Noni. What did you do?"

Noni averted her gaze for a split second and shrugged. "I ain't do nothing."

"So, you telling me you didn't do nothing all day yesterday?"

Wondering if Double-O had ratted her out, she shook her head. "Nah, not besides go holler at Teer like you told me to."

Asha knew she was lying. "Alright, well, that's what I want you to do until I get back."

Noni frowned, confused. "What you mean by that?"

"I mean, I don't want you doing nothing 'til I get back. You can watch movies, play your game, or whatever else that don't involve you leaving the house."

"Man, you tripping!" Noni protested. "'Cause I know you don't expect me to—"

"That's exactly what I expect you to do," Asha cut her off. "Since you wanna sit up here and act like didn't nothing happen yesterday. Like I'm calling you at four in the morning for no damn reason. I had a nightmare, Noni. So don't tell me didn't nothing happen. But like I said, sit your ass down 'til I get back."

"What about the pickups?"

"Let Double-O take care of that."

"Well, what if I wanna get something to eat?"

"Order it."

Angrily shaking her head, Noni mumbled something under her breath.

"I didn't hear you?" Asha turned her ear to the screen.

"Man, I said I'm 'bout to go back to bed."

"Alright, text me when you wake up."

Noni looked away and dryly replied, "Yeah, alright."

"Aye, Noni?" Asha called. When Noni looked up, Asha said, "Ain't there something you wanna tell me before you hang up?"

She sighed in irritation and grumbled, "I love you, twin."

Asha smiled. "I love you, too, girl. And I'll talk to you later."

Seconds after Asha disconnected the call, Lo-Lo entered the room.

"Damn, girl," Asha joked, "I bet your lil' nosy ass had that ear all over the door."

"And you know this." Lo-Lo laughed. "So, fill me in on the parts I don't know."

Vividly recalling her horrible dream, Asha verbally relived what had jolted her awake in a cold sweat.

After listening intently, Lo-Lo asked, "So what do you think it means?"

As Asha considered her suspicions that Dullah was responsible for her family's calamity, she turned to her girl and quietly confided, "I've been keeping a secret, love."

Lo-Lo reached for her hand and held it in comfort. "What is it?"

Explaining this was something they couldn't tell Noni, she told her about the meeting with Dullah at the restaurant. "...And he knew things that only me and Noni knew about. So that tells me he had to be involved, Lo'."

Lo-Lo wanted to pry, but instead she supportively replied, "You already know I stand behind whatever you wanna do. And I can understand why you'd be hesitant to tell Noni. 'Cause it ain't no secret how she gon' respond."

Asha nodded in agreement, thinking how they had come too far to just throw it all away. "But don't get me wrong, the nigga gotta get it. But I wanna make it happen to where it don't blow back on us. 'Cause he a maggot that definitely keep a flock of flies around him at all times."

Aware of Dullah's infatuation with Asha, Lo-Lo could only shake her head at the underlying motive behind his treacherous actions. He wanted Asha for a wife, and his twisted mind thought that by removing her mother from the picture it would bring them closer together. While she had always known he was a dangerous man, Lo-Lo morally shivered from the extent of his evilness.

As Asha and Lo-Lo continued to converse on the subject, Angel knocked on the door before entering the room. When she sensed the seriousness of whatever they were discussing, she offered an apology and turned to leave.

"Nah, you good," Asha spoke up. "I just had a bad dream, that's all."

"You okay?" Angel genuinely asked.

"Yeah, I'm alright. Just still can't believe how real it felt."

Angel joined them on the bed, unable to stifle a grin of excitement. "I hardly slept last night. 'Cause we really about to try and pull this off, ain't we?"

They nodded, with Lo-Lo asking her, "You been rehearsing your spiel? 'Cause once we press play, ain't no button to rewind."

"I have," Angel assured. "But I just still keep thinking we might need more time. 'Cause what if–"

"Stop!" Asha sternly cut her off. "Ain't no room for negative thinking right now. If we run into a problem, we'll handle it. But what we not gon' do is speak it into existence."

"And besides," Lo-Lo chimed in, "I don't think there's a man on earth who can outsmart three women on the same page. So as long as our presentation on point, this shit gon' be a walk in the park."

Fueled by Asha's logic and Lo-Lo's reasoning, Angel was determined to prove she was worthy of being a member of the Butterfly Mafia.

***

"Hopping out the foreign with the Louie slides, movie time/ go against the gang that's a suicide, don't do it slime/ never snitching, if I do the crime I'ma do the time/ never switching, if you forever loyal I'll forever ride."

On her bedroom floor in a sports bra and Nike shorts, Noni was vibing to Young M.A. while performing her morning exercise. And in spite of harboring an attitude toward Asha, she had still sent her a short text shortly after waking up.

Noni was on the verge of going to the shower when her phone buzzed on the bed from an incoming call. Backpedaling several steps, she looked at the screen and saw it was Double-O.

"What up doe?" Double-O greeted upon Noni answering the phone.

"Shit. What's good with you?"

"I'm 'bout to pull up. Come outside."

Rocking a gray hoodie - in which she had concealed her micro hellcat pistol, Noni had her hand on the knob of the front door, when she suddenly withdrew it. With Asha's oder not to leave the echoing in her ear, she called Double-O and told him to come in. "Cause I just got out the shower and I ain't trying to get sick."

Double-O and CJ gave Noni hugs and handshakes as she let them in. Eyeing her closely, Double-O felt that her energy was off. "Wassup with you?" He asked as they stood in the living room.

Not one to beat around the bush, Noni questioned, "Aye, did you talk to my sister last night or this morning?"

"Nah, why? Wassup?"

"'Cause she called my phone at like four this morning on some other shit. Like she knew what happened last night. And I'm just trying to figure out who would've told her."

"Well, it wasn't from my end. And CJ been with me since you dropped us off last night."

"And even if I wasn't with him," CJ spoke for himself, "I still would've kept my tongue in neutral if she would've called me."

Noni eyed them for a minute before deciding they were being truthful. She concluded that Asha's inquiry had been purely coincidental.

"So what y'all doing up this early?" She asked as they sat on opposite sofas.

Double-O leaned forward, "I think the nigga Smurf had something to do with that shit last night. And I'm also thinking your lil' mans was involved, too. 'Cause dog was acting real weird."

Recalling Pierre's strange behavior, Noni couldn't dispute Double-O's assumption. But because her and Pierre had been cool since adolescence, she couldn't help but wonder what he'd been given to play the role of Judas.

"Yeah, he was definitely tweaking," she admitted. "So that's probably who we need to start with. But after last night, I highly doubt the nigga in the projects right now."

Double-O smirked, "I know where the nigga Smurf laying his head at. So, lace up and let's roll."

Upon noticing a look of hesitation on Noni's face, Double-O added, "I've been in a lot of battles, my baby. And one of the main reasons I'm still breathing is my direct approach. I crush opps with a sense of urgency. 'Cause this game ain't based on heart, but whoever draw first."

Slightly offended by his implications, Noni assured him in a coarse tone, "Nigga, I kill with a clear conscious. So don't mistake my hesitation for no coward shit."

CJ curiously cut in, "Then what's the problem? Let's go get this nigga."

She briefly held his stare before she looked away and lied, "I got something going on right now. I can't leave."

"Why not?" CJ probed, peering toward her ankles for a sign of a house arrest monitor.

As Noni was reluctant to answer, Double-O's mind put the pieces together. He grinned at Noni. "You on punishment, ain't you?"

"Nigga, yeah right." She waved him off. "I'ma grown ass woman."

Double-O turned to CJ. "Bro, remember she just said Asha called her early this morning, tripping and shit. Now I'm willing bet a dollar to a dime that Asha done told her ass she better not go nowhere, no time soon."

"I ain't never heard of a goon getting grounded," CJ joked before they both busted out in laughter.

As the two cackling hyenas clutched their stomachs, Noni stood up from the sofa. "That shit wasn't even that funny. So y'all can take y'all corny ass on somewhere. 'Cause I really do need to take a shower."

"For what?" CJ cried. "You can't even go no-muthafucking-where!"

With his comment increasing the volume of their laughter, Noni went to the front door and opened it. But before she could throw them out, she was rendered speechless by the sight of two detectives who were standing on her porch.

Chapter 2

Hollywood, California...

Within a lively environment, Angel, Lo-Lo, and Asha were the center of attention as they occupied a VIP booth in a strip called called Déjà Vu. Along with buckets of top shelf champagne, their table was covered in currency—which they were currently inserting into money-gun dispensers.

When Rihanna's stripper anthem *Pour It Up* began blaring through the speakers, Angel led the way toward the center stage, where the three girls opened fire on the dancers with a barrage of bills.

Observing the exhibit from across the room were two heartless felons who were natives of Compton. They'd been watching the three women since their magnetic arrival, suspecting the Mexican of being the leader.

"Cuz, is you witnessing this shit?" one of the killers said to his comrade. "Nigga, them hoes just shot out at least ten bands."

Wearing a thoughtful expression as he stroked his goatee, the man named Bluefish bobbed his head in acknowledgement. With the words "RIP TOOKIE" tattooed over the left brow of his wide-set eyes, Bluefish was notorious by nature and a hustler by trade. And he was almost positive he was presently peering at the prospect of prosperity. Once the song ended and the girls returned to their booth, Bluefish called on his comrade to join him. "Come on, Loc, we 'bout to introduce 'em to this Compton shit." By means of their signature West Coast shuffle, they approached the girls' booth with upturned chins. "I'm Bluefish," the towering thug extended his hand to Angel. "And this the homie, Big Feez."

"I'm Angie," Angel lied with a bright smile. "And these my best friends, Tasha and Lori."

After an exchange of handshakes, Bluefish locked eyes with Angel and asked, "So how come I've never seen you here before? 'Cause with a face like yours, I know I wouldn't forget it."

"You come here that often?" she teasingly replied.

Impressed by her quick-witted reply, he shrugged. "Shit, 'til I meet wifey, then this what it is."

"That's understandable," Angel nodded. "But to answer your question, the reason you've never seen me is because I'm not from around here. My girls flew in from the Midwest, and I'm just showing them a good time."

"Where y'all from?" Feez joined the conversation, looking at both Asha and Lo-Lo. They were equally attractive, which made it hard to decide on who to pursue.

"We from Chicago," Lo-Lo volunteered. "And y'all?"

"We from Compton. Santana Blocc."

"Oh, so you Loc'd out, huh?" Lo-Lo smiled.

"What you know about that?" Feez smirked in amusement.

"I just told you we from the Chi'. That's the motherland of that gang shit. I could probably put you up on lit'."

"Yeah, well, I'm more into finances now. So, if you familiar with that, I'm all ears."

Favoring the late legend Nipsey Hussle, Feez still flew his flag high, but was now more concerned with collecting coins than kills. His mindset was in sync with the lyrics *'if you can't get money on a earth this big, you worthless kid'*. So having convinced Bluefish to join him on a less dangerous, but prosperous journey, the two friends were in desperate search of a cocaine connect.

Angel invited them into the booth but warned, "That's only if y'all can hang. Cause as you see, it's still plenty money and even more champagne."

Whereas Bluefish literally leaped next to Angel, Feez faltered before finally planting himself between Asha and Lo-Lo. "I know a big Crip out of Compton can handle two twenty-three-year-olds," Lo-Lo purred in Feez's ear.

As his manhood awakened in anticipation, Feez put an arm around both girls and cockily assured, "If I don't make both y'all tap out, then Popeye a bitch."

"So, you still ain't told me where you from?" Bluefish said to Angel, drinking champagne directly from the bottle.

"I'm originally from Mexico, but my family came to Chicago when I was young. Then I got married right out of high school, and my husband moved me out here to Malibu."

"What a happily married woman doing up in Déjà Vu?" he tested.

"Who said I was happily married?" Angel took a sip of Ciroc.

"I'm saying, a woman as gorgeous as you, it's gotta be something keeping you around. Clearly you could have any man you want."

Angel eyed him as if weighing whether or not he was trustworthy, then leaned closer to quietly confide, "It would be foolish of me to leave a man who's the Capo of a cartel, you don't think?"

Unable to restrain his growing excitement, Bluefish casually inquired, "So what you saying, your husband the 'plug' or something?"

Angel shook her head and stamped with authority. "Nah, I'm saying he the *socket*."

Bluefish suddenly had an outbreak of goosebumps. This was the opportunity him and Feez had been prayerfully awaiting. And who would've thought their prayer would be answered in the booth of a strip club.

Before Bluefish could thirstily present a proposal, Angel beat him to the punch and said, "I can see the wheels in your mind turning. But right now, I just wanna kick it with my girls and have a good time." Placing her lips near his ear, she added in a sultry tone, "My husband away on business. So, if you play your cards right, maybe we can get better acquainted."

In the midst of Feez flirting with Asha and Lo-Lo, he caught eyes with Bluefish and slipped him a wink. It wasn't often you encountered young beautiful women who were eager to splurge.

"So, what y'all doing after this?" Asha asked Feez, laying a hand on his thigh.

"Shit, it's whatever, you feel me. Why wassup, what y'all got in mind?"

"Something a little more private, if you feel where I'm coming from."

Feez shrugged. "Say less then."

After drowning their kidneys in cognac and helping the girls donate ever dollar to the appreciative dancers, Bluefish and Feez drunkenly trailed them outside.

Angel slightly staggered before grabbing Bluefish for support. "I don't even know you," she purposely slurred, "so why is something telling me you're of the real ones? Am I wrong about you, Bluefish, baby?"

He moistened his lips and declared from the core of his heart, "I wasn't sworn in it, I was born in it, baby girl. I live by loyalty, and I'ma die by a code that's exposed the weakness in many men. So, trust me. To give me a chance would be beneficial to us both."

Angel studied his eyes in deliberation, then playfully challenged, "You know how to Crip Walk?"

"As if I was Sugar Bear herself," he replied, referring to the woman who invented the dance.

"Gone and hit that shit for 'em, Cuz," Feez encouraged him.

As if he was moving to music, Bluefish began skipping with a skill that would've made Snoop take notes. When he ended the dance by dusting his shoes, the girls cheered in delight and applauded his performance.

"Alright, player, you did that," Angel admitted. "But now let's see if y'all can really keep up."

Bluefish and Feez exchanged a look as the girls walked off and hopped in a Bentley Bentayga.

Lo-Lo pulled up alongside them and Angel lowered her window, "Follow us... Loc."

Smirking in response, Bluefish and Feez marched to a Royal blue Impala on shiny gold wheels.

As they chased the truck down the interstate at 90 mph, Bluefish reached beneath his seat and came up holding a chrome handgun.

"Wassup, Cuz?" Feez briefly took his eyes off the road to regard the revolver.

"Shit, just in case they think shit sweet. We ain't going out like no marks, homie."

When they arrived at the mansion in Malibu, parked in its circular driveway was a S550 Benz and a hot pink Lamborghini. Mentally calculating the cost of all three luxury vehicles, Bluefish and Feez knew they'd hit a lick so few had experienced. And they intended to take full advantage.

Angel asked them to remove their shoes as they entered the house. "I got custom flooring that ran me a fortune."

While being given a tour of the lower level, Bluefish didn't fail to take notice of the framed pictures on the walls. Taken in scenic locations, they were photographs of Angel and an older man.

When she led Bluefish up the spiral staircase and into the master suite, he couldn't resist from reaching for a picture on the nightstand. "So, this the lucky man, huh?" he asked while studying the hardened eyes of the older Hispanic.

"Yes, that's him," Angel confirmed, plucking the picture from his hand and returning it to its original place. "But if that's who I wanted to think about right now, I'd call him."

"So, what's on your mind?" he took a step closer and encircled his arms around her waist.

"For starters, what's your real name?"

"Oooh." Bluefish groaned. "You going deep out the gate."

"Life short, so why waste time in what we both know coming. So, tell me, what's on your birth certificate?"

"Some wild shit."

"Try me."

"Dydreekus," he shyly revealed.

"Yeah, that's definitely different. But I've heard worse. And for the record, my real name Angelina."

Through further questioning, she learned that Bluefish was 27 years old, had been around the gang life since infancy, and had recently acquired an appetite for something other than drive-bys and bitched robberies.

"I don't put in more *work* than most of my OGs," Bluefish truthfully stated. "But besides stripes I can't take to no bank and get a loan with, that shit ain't put nothing in my pockets but gunshot residue."

"I hear you," Angel replied. "I really do. And I wouldn't mind helping you, 'cause I sense you've been through a lot. But you gotta understand that right now I'm living in the moment. I'm not trying to fuck up my marriage."

"And I ain't asking you to. We can be discreet, while adding value to each other at the same time. Cause in the end, that's what all relationships should be about anyway. I'ma hood nigga, no doubt, but what I've learned is that when dealing with people, they either pushing or pulling."

Angel inhaled a deep breath and slowly exhaled. "Listen, I can't make no promises, but I'll see what I can do. My husband definitely won't deal with a new face, but I'll see if I can get you in with my girl, Lori's, brother. Him and my husband have a monthly arrangement, so I'll try and pull a few strings that way. But don't hold me to it."

Bluefish picked her up and grinned. "I swear I'ma show you how a real Compton nigga get down. And I ain't talking none of that rapping shit. This here real life."

"But there's just one condition." Angel smiled.

"Name it."

"You gotta show me how to do that dance."

Her phone buzzed in her back pocket, and she told Bluefish to put her down. When she saw who the call was from, she put a finger to her lips for Bluefish to be quiet. "Hey, honey," Angel answered in a cheerful voice. She was listening to the caller and suddenly looked up at Bluefish in panic. "Alright, I'll see you soon. I love you, too." Immediately upon disconnecting the call she announced that her husband was on his way home from the airport. Pulling Bluefish along, Angel raced downstairs in search of the others, who were out back in the swimming pool. "Come on y'all gotta go!" Angel yelled frantically at Feez, gathering up his clothes. "My husband on the way."

"What?" Lo-Lo shrieked in alarm, as she quickly hopped out the pool and began drying off. "Are you serious?"

"Yes, girl. The man just called from the airport."

As Feez quickly got dressed, Angel looked around before asking, "Where Tasha at?"

"She ran to go pray to that porcelain god," Lo-Lo answered, slipping into her jeans. "You know that girl ain't no drinker for real."

Angel hurriedly ushered the two men around to their car, where Bluefish paused before hopping in. "We still good on that, right?"

"Yes!" she answered, nervously scanning the area for a nosy neighbor. "Now, please, go before you get me in a world of trouble. Then there won't be nothing I can do for you."

As Feez reversed the Impala out onto the street and sped off, Bluefish tilted his head upwards and erupted in laughter. "Cuz, we 'bout to be the kings of Compton!"

Chapter 3

After being interrogated by the two homicide detectives, Noni was released from custody with a promise that her movements would be closely monitored. Exiting the precinct, she reached for her phone to call Double-O, when the backseat window of a white sedan lowered.

"Get in," Perez instructed with a nudge of his head.

Despite being surprised and leery, Noni masked her emotions and confidently climbed in. "How you know where I was at?" she asked as the Maybach moved away from the curb.

"I have associates from all walks of life," Perez replied, removing his aviator frames. "And I can't begin to tell you how important that is, if a person wishes to maintain their position at the pinnacle."

"So, what? You had your peoples pick me up to see if I would talk?" The detectives' line of questioning had centered around the triple murder she'd committed on the drug lord's behalf. But with the code of silence embedded in her heart, Noni had unwaveringly answered, "I don't know what you talking about."

Perez peered in her eyes and lied without blinking, "If I was concerned about you having loose lips, I'd just throw you off the ship before you had a chance to sink it."

Noni didn't take kind to his threat but kept her tongue in check. "Yeah, well, I ain't got nothing to worry about no way.

'Cause I ain't have nothing to do with nothing. They chasing they tail."

"Even still, you need to exercise caution," Perez counseled. "Because someone clearly pointed them in your direction."

Noni considered members of her clan before ruling them out. Regardless of what Perez said, she was certain he was responsible for the intense interrogation.

"So, what's the deal between you and my little sister?" he nosily inquired as they idled at a stop light.

"I don't kiss and tell. That's something you gotta take up with her."

"I'm only asking because I feel anything romantic would be a mistake, in light of our new business arrangement. It could lead to a conflict of interest."

Noni was hardly surprised when the Maybach's driver turned down the street on which she lived. This was just another way of Perez displaying the extent his reach and resources.

"I know Angel's an adult, but she's the only sister I got," Perez said as Noni opened the back door. "So, whatever she's involved in, know that I'm holding you responsible for her wellbeing."

As Noni watched the car pull off, she could help wondering if dealing with Angel would turn out fatal.

***

California

"We need to link up," Angel told Bluefish over speakerphone, while getting dressed. Over the past several days they'd been regularly communicating through Facetime and texts.

"When?"

"Now. I can have my driver bring me to you."

"A'ight, come through. I'm in Compton." While Bluefish could've easily met her someplace else, he wanted his peers to peep him being picked up by a pretty Hispanic.

Chauffeured by two hired security guards, Angel arrived in Compton by way of a custom SUV. From behind its tinted windows, she observed the inquisitive stares of pedestrians as the tank-size truck pushed through the most unsafe section of Los Angeles. When they pulled up to the address Bluefish had given her, there were a number of heavily tattooed men standing in the front yard. As some sported royal blue bandanas from their left back pockets, they eyed the truck as if it was packed with Pirus.

Angel sent Bluefish a text to let him she was outside.

He emerged from the house minutes later, rocking a proud grin and powder blue fabrics. This was the most important he'd felt in a long time.

On cue, the passenger of the truck stepped out to open the back door for Bluefish, which offered the ogling offenders a brief view of Angel's olive complexion.

"West up, baby girl?" Bluefish greeted as he slid in beside her and the guard closed the door.

"I'm good. And you?"

"Shit, much better, now that I'm in your presence. You gotta energy I can't explain."

Angel pressed a button to raise the privacy partition. "I was able to get you in. But for no more than eight kilos. But with its quality, you won't have a problem doubling them up."

Eight of 'em, he nervously thought to himself. He wasn't expecting to cop that many, which was definitely beyond his budget. "And what's the ticket?" he couldn't help but inquire.

"If you give your word to be a consistent buyer, you can get them for just twenty-thousand a piece."

Bluefish nodded, already racking his brain for a way to attain additional funds. This was an opportunity that came only once in a lifetime.

"However," Angel added, "if you're not ready or uncertain, there's no pressure. You asked me to put you in the game and that's what I did. So, the ball in your court now, Bluefish, baby."

If he was to pull this off, there was only one seeable alternative; he'd have to invite other people to the table. As much as he hungered for all the glory, common sense convinced him to eat as a team.

"How soon I gotta give you the money?" he asked. "'Cause I gotta go all the way out to Sacramento and get it from my Granny house. A nigga can't have that type of cash laying around in Compton. These niggas killing for crumbs, you feel me."

"No later than the weekend. But it could happen as early as Thursday. When playing at this level, you'll learn that giving specific times and dates can be very dangerous."

He bobbed his head in understanding. "A'ight, I'ma take care of it. But just so I ain't all the way in the blind, where we gon' handle the exchange?"

"At my house. And you can meet Lori's brother yourself."

Thinking this was too good to be true, Bluefish reached over to palm one of her legging-clad thighs. "I know it's said you shouldn't mix business with pleasure, but I believe there's an exception for every rule. You should let me express my gratitude." He lowered his gaze and lustfully informed, "And I'm known for cleaning my plate."

Angel shivered, as if she was tempted to indulge. "Rather than make plans, let's just let whatever happens happen. It can make an experience even more exciting."

Promising to be in touch, Angel dismissed him with a kiss on the cheek.

After watching the truck disappear down the block, Bluefish turned to walk through the crowd of his curious comrades.

"Damn, Cuz, who the fuck was that?" several of them asked.

"The plug," he cockily answered before entering the house. With him and Feez having only $76,000 combined, Bluefish had some serious calls to make. He just had to be sure to disguise his desperation.

Three Days Later...

With Feez behind the wheel of a less conspicuous car, he turned in the driveway of Angel's Malibu mansion. Beside him Bluefish cradled a backpack that contained $160,000.

It had taken only a few calls for Bluefish to secure the funds. It largely helped that the news of Angel's appearance had spread like wildfire. Assuring his investors he'd return their money with interest, Bluefish was told to come pick it up.

Wedging a weapon in his waistband before exiting the car, Bluefish followed Feez to the front door. They paid no attention to the Bentley truck as they strode toward the house.

Angel opened the door as they walked up. "Hey." She greeted Bluefish with a kiss on the cheek as they came inside.

"Damn, what's that smell?" he asked, inhaling a mouthwatering aroma that came from the kitchen.

"I made some steak and potatoes. I was thinking I could feed you a home cooked meal before you leave. You know, being as though you like to clean your plate."

As they exchanged a knowing grin, Feez frowned. "Fuck is y'all on?"

"Chill, Cuz. This grown man business, homie."

Angel was leading them through the house, when a young white dude announced from the top of the staircase, "I'm almost done, Angie."

"Alright, I'll be up there in a minute."

As she sat Bluefish and Feez beneath a sunshade table in the backyard, Angel nudged her head at the backpack and asked if it was all there.

"The whole one-sixty," he proudly answered, holding it out for her to take.

"Okay, I'ma let him run it through a counter real quick, then I'ma call for you. And make sure to let him know this is just the beginning. Because loyalty goes a long way in this line of work."

When Angel went inside, Bluefish beamed at Feez in triumph. "Cuz, we bout to go back to the 'hood with bricks. Eight of them bitches!"

As they shook up in celebration, Feez boasted, "That's that 'Tana shit, Loc."

The two men were discussing future plans and intentions, when Feez glanced at his watch. "Cuz, we been out here like twenty minutes. How long it take to run that shit through a money counter?"

Injected with alarm, Bluefish rose from the table and withdrew his weapon. "I don't know. But I'm finna find out," he said before marching into the house.

With Feez on his heels, Bluefish yelled Angel's name while descending the staircase two steps at a time. Upon reaching the top landing, he saw the white dude coming out the bathroom, toting a toolbox.

"Aye, where the fuck Angie at?" Bluefish growled through clenched teeth.

Noticing the gun in the inquirers hand, the man nervously stuttered, "She-she-she said she had to run to the store real quick, and she'd be right back."

Bluefish grabbed him by his shirt and jammed the gun under his chin. "Nigga, if you don't give me my muthafucking money, I'ma blow yo' shit off!"

"I don't know nothing about no money." He threw his hands up in surrender. I'm just a plumber."

As a wild-eyed Bluefish contemplated on whether or not to squeeze, Feez began looking around as something dawned on him. "Aye, hold up," he told Bluefish. "Let me check something real quick."

Feez went downstairs and returned moments later with disheartening news. "Cuz, it ain't a picture of that bitch nowhere in sight no more."

Warning the plumber not to move, Bluefish went to the master bedroom, where he noticed the framed photo of Angie and her husband was no longer present. *Ain't no way*, Bluefish panicked to himself as he flew out the room and raced downstairs. He snatched open the front door and was just in time to see a flatbed pull in the driveway. He approached the driver as he hopped out the truck. "What's going on, my man?"

"I'm here to return these vehicles to the rental agency."

"A rental agency?" Bluefish repeated in sheer disbelief.

The man held up a form. "Yeah, if you look right here, it lists a hot pink Lam—"

Bluefish tuned him out as he turned to walk away.

With his heart having sunk to the soles of his feet, Bluefish realized he'd been the victim of a cold finesse. He had allowed three women that lived who knows where to swindle him of his entire life savings. Not to mention the money borrowed from investors who'd show no sympathy.

As he went to fetch Feez and feed him the foul-tasting news, Bluefish looked towards the heavens and began laughing hysterically. For he felt this just had to be a sick joke played by God Himself.

***

Arriving at LAX, Angel, Lo-Lo and Asha exited the Bentley with their carry-on luggage. Each wearing oversized shades, they marched to a private jet that Lo-Lo had chartered with one of the phony credit cards.

As they were led up the short flight of steps and shown to the jet's luxurious cabin, Lo-Lo removed her shades to leisurely take in the beautiful enclosure. This being a surreal moment she'd never forget, she grabbed Asha and lovingly squeezed her.

Filled with confidence from her crafty accomplishment, Angel plopped down on a seat and kicked up her feet. "Just me being truthful, that shit was a lot easier than I thought. I guess I never knew a man could be so gullible." She looked over at their luggage and smirked. "The power of illusion."

Inside their carry-on luggage was the $160,000, along with the pictures of Angel and her deceased father. She had considered using photos of her and Perez, but with her father already gone, there was only one way for Bluefish to ever bump into him.

The plane was ascending into the clouds, when Asha sat next to Angel and quietly counseled, "You did good, but you gotta stay humble, love. 'Cause the second we get too cocky is when the universe will force-feed us a slice of its humble pie. And there can't be no happy endings with an upset stomach."

While en route to their next destination, the girls were sipping wine and discussing ways to polish their performance. For in just a few short hours they'd be landing in Miami where they would finesse another fool with the same illusion.

A week later...

Outside Detroit international, Noni was leaning against the back of an SUV as Asha, Lo-Lo and Angel exited the airport. She rose off the truck when they got within arm's reach and embraced each girl, ending with Angel.

"Did you miss me?" Angel asked as they disengaged.

In answer, Noni drew her succulent lips into a sensuous kiss.

Lo-Lo stuck her head out the back passenger window. "Will y'all take y'all horny asses to a hotel and let's go!"

As Noni sped out the airport, she glanced over at Asha, who was staring out her window. "Wassup, twin, you good?"

Asha simply nodded in response.

Noni observed her a minute longer, then turned to look over her shoulder at Lo-Lo. "So how much y'all get?"

Unsure of what had altered Asha's mood, Lo-Lo downplayed her excitement and cooly replied. "A little over three hundred-thousand dollars."

"Damn, for real?" Noni exclaimed. "I mean, clearly I wasn't there, so fill me in on what happened."

Lo-Lo cut her eyes at Asha before subbing in Angel. "I mean, it was really Angel who put it down. So, she can paint a better picture than me."

Knowing she'd been thrown under the bus, Angel feigned fatigue and told Noni they could discuss it later. "'Cause, girl, I'm tired as hell. I just wanna go home, take a long bath and crawl in bed."

Noni scoffed, for she knew their evasiveness was based on Asha's energy. "You know what, don't even worry about it." She angrily squeezed the wheel. "'Cause y'all on some weird shit, anyway."

After dropping off Lo-Lo and Angel at their respective houses, Noni hopped on the highway and headed home. As she drove in silence, she couldn't help but wonder what her sister was thinking. Besides telling the girls she'd talk to them later, Asha hadn't spoken one other word. But other than being taken to the precinct for questioning, Noni hadn't left the house. So, she knew it couldn't be her.

Subsequent to circling the block, Noni pulled in their driveway and parked behind the GTO. She was on the verge of speaking, when Asha abruptly grabbed her luggage and exited the truck.

Hesitantly trailing her twin in the house, Noni closed the front door and locked it. Upon her turning around she was caught off guard when Asha slapped her. Grabbing her stinging cheek, Noni was frozen in shock. This being the first time her sister had ever hit her, her brain had yet to relay a reaction.

"Girl, don't you ever ignore my texts again!" Asha pointed, referring to Noni's neglectful behavior from two weeks prior. "I don't give a fuck how mad you are at me. Don't you ever worry me like that again, Noni. I had a nightmare. I was so afraid, and it felt it so real. And all I could think about was me not being there." Tears began falling from Asha's eyes as she continued to release her pent-up emotions.

And before long, Noni's uncommon connection with her twin sibling had her in tears as well. "I'm sorry, twin," she apologized, shamefully lowering her head. She was the cause of her sister's inner turmoil, and it pierced her heart with pangs of guilt.

Asha puller her sister into a fierce embrace. "I love you so much," she cried into Noni's hair. "You my little baby. And you all I got. And I'm sorry, too, 'cause I should've took you with me. And I promise not to ever leave you again. You hear me?"

Noni nodded, soaking Asha's shirt with unstoppable tears. She loved Asha just as much and had missed her dearly during their two-week separation.

The twins held on to each other until eventually regaining control of their emotions. With their noses running as they broke apart, both girls started giggling, then used their thumbs to dry each other's cheeks.

"We standing here like two big babies." Asha smiled as they blew their noses.

"Double-O said we the most emotional women he ever met." Noni laughed in recollection.

After another long hug and apology, Asha went to take a shower. She came out wearing a pajama outfit Noni had got her for Christmas and joined her sister in bed. "What you watching?"

"A movie by a dude named Ca$h," Noni answered without looking away from the screen. "He wrote books and shit in the joint, and now the nigga out doing movies."

Halfway through them watching *Till My Casket Drop*, Noni paused it and turned to Asha with a curious grin. "So, how easy was it to finesse them niggas for all that money?"

Recalling Bluefish from Compton, and a man named Baldy from Miami, Asha smirked. "Twin, that shit was easier than taking toys from toddlers. I swear, if women really knew how much more advanced we are than men, we'd have a woman President right now."

At having a sudden thought, Asha hopped out of bed and ran downstairs. She came back with the carry-on and sat it on the bed. Unzipping it, she turned it upside down and bundles of cash tumbled onto the comforter. "That's what three hundred and twenty-thousand dollars look like!"

Noni marvelled at the money, then looked up at her big sister in admiration. "You the truth, love. And I couldn't ask for a better twin."

From their thriving trap house to the accomplishment of their latest endeavor, there was no denying that Asha's brain was powered by wires of womanly wisdom.

"So, what you think it mean?" she asked Asha.

Because she had yet to inform Noni of Dullah's betrayal, Asha had to choose her words carefully. "I don't think it means Double-O a snake, but I do think it means somebody close to us could try to do us harm. So, we gotta stay on point."

With the guilt of her keeping a secret from Asha weighing on her conscious, Noni confessed, "Something did happen that night when you called." She then went on to tell her about the encounter with Pierre and Smurf, and the shootout that ensued shortly after.

Aside from being somewhat upset with Noni for not coming clean sooner, Asha couldn't believe that her dream had occurred on the same night as the incident. A disbeliever of coincidence, this was further verification that her and her twin shared a special connection.

"And there's something else," Noni continued.

As she explained how she'd been picked up for questioning, and Perez was waiting for her outside the precinct, Asha couldn't believe her ears. "Did he admit to having it done?" she asked, as her brain was arranging pieces.

"Nah, he acted like he didn't, but I know he did. Then he got to asking me about Angel. Talking 'bout how me messing with her ain't good for business. But I ain't gon' lie, I was lightweight hot when he pulled up to our crib. Like he letting me know he can touch us whenever."

When considering Perez's caliber and connections, Asha was hardly surprised that he knew where they lived. In fact, that was something she had already anticipated. But that didn't mean she didn't have a counter move in the making.

"Alright, so this what we gon' do," Asha began. "First, we gon' address that situation with Pierre and old buddy, 'cause I gotta feeling it's all tied to Dullah. And far as Perez, don't say nothing to Angel about, 'cause we don't need them feuding over no frivolous shit."

"So how you want me to play it with her?" Noni asked, secretly hoping she wasn't asking her to sever emotional ties.

Asha eyed her closely. "What, you done caught feelings already?"

Noni shrugged. "I mean, she cool. But I wouldn't say all that. You know where my heart at."

"Noni, don't let lust blind you to the bigger picture. And remember, our butterfly only got four wings. So it's cool to have friends, but ain't no room for more family."

Chapter 4

"Alright, I'll see you in a few days, Rev'." Asha shook hands with Reverend Daniels as they stood outside his Church. "And again, I just wanna say thank you for helping me. And not that I'm into keeping secrets from my people, but I'm hoping we can keep this between us."

He nodded in understanding. "I hear you, little sister. And for whatever it's worth, I'll be praying for you. The Most High gave me the ability to read eyes, and in yours I see a troubled soul with great responsibility. But may you always remember, He gives the toughest battles to only His toughest soldiers. If you wasn't built to win, you wouldn't have made it this far. So, keep striving, little sister. And when the student is ready, the teacher shall appear."

The Reverend's words continued to resonate in Asha's mind as she drove to her next destination. Whether or not she was destined to succeed in life was a question she often considered. So, for someone who hardly knew her to speak such things could only mean she was moving along the correct course.

But does God really see me as one of His toughest soldiers? she found herself wondering as she wheeled into the parking lot of a PNC bank.

Toting a designer handbag, Asha entered the bank where her and Noni kept their savings and met with the manager. This was one of the most important meetings of her life.

After being greeted by the manager with a firm handshake, she was led to his office and directed to have a seat.

"So, Ms. Kincaid, I understand you wanted to propose a business plan of some sort," he said from a seated position behind his neatly arranged desk.

"I do." Asha nodded, removing paperwork from inside her handbag. "It's a three-year plan, and there's no doubt in my mind it'll unfold exactly as I predict. All I need is one chance, sir, and I give you my word I won't let you down."

He was scanning the pages of her business plan, when he inquired without looking up, "Which college do you attend, Ms. Kincaid?"

"Wayne State," she answered, curious as to what had prompted the question. If she were a reader of minds, she would've known that he was actually impressed by the professionalism of her plan.

"And how old are you again?"

"I'll be twenty-one in August."

He nodded, as if her age is what concerned him. "Ms. Kincaid, I can tell by the language in your plan that you're a bright young lady. But the amount of money you're seeking is a risk I'm not sure the bank would be willing to take. This would be your first business venture. And we can't just shell out money to everyone with high hopes."

Having anticipated the direction in which the meeting would go, Asha had come thoroughly prepared. For the livelihood of her team depended on it.

Asha grabbed the handbag and leaned forward to set it on his desk.

He eyed it in confusion before looking up at her. "I don't understand."

"You will if you open it."

Upon doing so, his eyes widened at the sight of what was inside.

"That's over three hundred thousand dollars," Asha informed him, "which means, technically, I have enough to cover the loan. Mr. Fowler, I just need you to push the paperwork through. And as token of my gratitude..." She plucked a payoff from the bag and tossed it on the desk. As he studied the bribe in confliction, Asha reasoned, "Sir, I'm not asking you to break the law or put your job in jeopardy. I'm simply asking for a chance. And I'm fully aware that we live in a society where favors are often exchanged."

After a lapse of thoughtful silence on Mr. Fowler's part, he rose from his desk as a sign that the meeting was over. "Let me think it over and I'll be in touch."

Although the loan had yet to be approved, Asha left the bank with a euphoric feeling; for the manager had made no effort to return the payoff.

Flint, Michigan

"Hi, pretty baby!" Asha beamed, as she scooped up Polaris and gave her an affectionate squeeze. While she doubted she'd ever have a child of her own, this little girl gave Asha a glimpse of the joy a child brought to their parent.

"There's gotta be something about you," D'Aura said as they went into the apartment, with Asha carrying the baby in her arms. "Because I've never seen her take to someone as quickly as she did to you."

"It's 'cause she know I'ma child at heart," Asha said before tickling Polaris and causing her to laughingly squirm.

"So how was the trip?" D'Aura asked, as Asha sat the child on the living room floor to play with her toys.

"Girllll..." She smiled, reaching over to grasp D'Aura's forearm. "Let's just say that when it comes to a woman who can use her brain, a nigga don't stand a chance. We'll run circles around that ass!"

Also smiling, D'Aura bobbed her head in agreement. "And why do you think that is?"

"Because the average man controlled by that brainless thing between his legs. Think about it, he can have a loyal woman who'll give him the world, but he'll still risk it all for another woman who don't gotta loyal bone in her whole body. Now if that ain't weakness wrapped up in stupidity, then I don't know what is."

As she reflected on the reason behind the failed relationship between her and her child's father, D'Aura could definitely attest to the truthfulness of Asha's statement. For she had served that man her soul on a platter- with her mind, body, and heart as the sides; but it wasn't enough.

"How you looking on funds?" Asha asked, reaching in her purse.

D'Aura pulled Asha's hand from the purse. "If you don't stop. I still got over half of what you gave me from last time."

"You sure? 'Cause I promise you it's not a problem. And there's plenty more where it came from."

"Asha, I'm positive, girl. I appreciate it, but you've done more than enough."

D'Aura had purchased Polaris some new clothes and toys, picked up household items, and deposited the rest in her savings for a rainy day. Although the money had come without effort, she would treat it as if it was hard-earned.

Asha was both pleased and relieved by D'Aura's reaction; for the offering had been a test, and her refusal revealed the the quality of her character. She was not the type to take advantage of kindness.

"Remember I said I needed to talk to you when I got back?" Asha asked, to which D'Aura nodded. "Well, listen, I'm on the verge of opening up a business. I already applied for the loan, and I'm pretty sure it's gon' get approved. So I'm saying, is you trying to come and work with me or what?"

As D'Aura gave it thought, Asha persuasively inserted, "And just so you know, I'ma triple whatever you making at your job right now."

That got D'Aura's attention. "But you don't even know how much I'm making."

"It don't matter." Asha shrugged. "I can cover it. I just need to know if you on board."

D'Aura eyed her with an earnest expression. "I can't get caught up in nothing illegal, Asha. As bad as I wanna get ahead, I can't do it at the expense of losing my daughter, girl."

In spite of being mildly offended, Asha understood the woman's concern. Besides her child, everyone else had probably used her to their advantage. So D'Aura couldn't help but be skeptical of such an invitation.

Taking D'Aura's hand in her own, Asha peered directly into her eyes and stated, "It would go against everything I stood for if I was to purposely put you or your child in harm's way. You got every right to refuse my offer, but understand that I'm only trying to help you. And to surround myself with a pure-hearted woman would be helping me as well."

D'Aura regarded the younger woman with a subtle smile. "If they made more like you, the world would be a much better place."

"So does that mean you on board?" Asha grinned.

"Girl, do you know how much driving that'll be? Going back and forth from here to Detroit, every day."

"Yeah, that's why I've already been looking for you a nice spot in the city. And if you give me the word, I'ma pay the rent for the next six months."

D'Aura shook her head in amazement. "What I'ma do with you?"

As the wheels of her mind sensibly spun, D'Aura studied her daughter for a minute before turning to Asha and nodding her head. "A'ight, I'm in. But you don't gotta pay me triple. I'll earn my up."

"Double or nothing," Asha seriously countered.

"Well, if you insist." D'Aura laughed, leaning over to embrace who she believed to be an angel on earth.

"Mama, can we go to McDonald's?" Polaris walked up, holding her hands behind her back in a gesture of innocence.

D'Aura looked at Asha and joked. "Girl, you see what I gotta deal with?"

"I ain't even gon' lie to you." Asha laughed. "With a face like hers, she'd have my butt driving her to McDonald's on a regular basis."

After encouraging D'Aura to "take that baby to McDonald's", Asha checked the time and said she had to get back on the road.

"A'ight, girl." D'Aura hugged her at the door. "Drive careful and be sure to call me soon as you make it home."

"Bye, Asha!" Polaris waved, wearing the most adorable expression.

"Little girl, you gon' make me kidnap you." Asha bent down to give her a hug.

D'Aura laughed. "Why go through all that when you can just take her with you right now?"

They two women hugged again before Asha walked off.

As D'Aura closed the door and locked it, she had no way of knowing her affiliation with Asha would come at a costly price she'd be unable to afford.

Chapter 5

The Hemi of a Hellcat was howling as the car sped through the darkened streets of Detroit. Behind its 5% tint, CJ was bobbing his head to Tee Grizzley as he handled the wheel with a skillful ease. Beside him was a focused Double-O, who wore dark clothing and a solemn appearance. He always went mute moments before a murder, as his mind would imagine every possible scenario.

When reaching the west side, CJ turned down a residential street and Double-O slid lower in his seat. Taking in the Silverado pickup that sat in front of a two-story house, they circled the block before parking across from the house in question.

Following the liquor-store shootout, Noni insisted they find Pierre, who she firmly believed was the source of its orchestration. But after days of combing the city, the weasel was nowhere to be found. So, they settled for their former friend, Smurf who happened to reside at the house in question.

"Bro, you know I ain't never been no hater," CJ quietly spoke, "but after the way this disloyal-ass nigga played me, I want my face to be the last one he see before he take that trip."

Double-O considered his words before replying, "If that's how it unfold, he all yours, my baby. But don't let your emotions cause you to jump the gun."

Before relieving Smurf of his most prized possession-that being his life, Double-O and CJ were given specific instructions to question the puppet in regard to the person who ordered the assassination attempt on Noni. Although the twins were certain it was Dullah pulling the strings, they wanted to be sure there were unknown foes.

Ten minutes into their stakeout, when Double-O's instincts would ultimately save their lives. Glancing at his side mirror on a hunch, he saw a hooded demon creeping toward the car in a crouched position. With no choice but to run, he barked for CJ to get out the car and followed behind him like a quarterback sneak.

A split second later came the crackle of rapid gunfire that lit up the night like the 4th of July. Courtesy of a switch attachment, which converted a Glock into a fully automatic, the demon let off thirty rounds with a single squeeze.

Lower to the ground than lizards, Double-O and CJ scrambled across the street and took cover behind a green Ford Fusion. Shards of shattered glass rained down over their heads as Hotrod was bent on turning them both into candle-lit vigils.

But before he had a chance to reload, Double-O rose up and began playing his favorite music— heavy metal.

As Hotrod was forced to get on defense and duck alongside the bullet-riddled Hellcat, Double-O grabbed CJ's arm and backpedaled between two houses. The cemetery was crammed with reckless warriors, and he was in no hurry to join them.

When Hotrod popped up in preparation to return fire, a gray coupe sped up. "Come on!" the driver, Dogbite, barked through the lowered window. "They ran through some houses!"

As they crept down the next block, scanning the area for signs of fleeing figures, Hotrod cursed in frustration at his failure to fulfill his promise to Mecca.

After Smurf's botched attempt on Noni's life, Mecca knew it was only a matter of time before the twins appeared on his doorstep. So, to not only prevent Smurf from squealing like a pig, but to also set a trap, Mecca ordered Hotrod to murder Smurf first; then simply wait for twins to show up. Other than Hotrod's misstep, it had been a clever plan.

"What you wanna do?" Dogbite asked as they idled at a stop sign. With the runners nowhere in sight, and two dead bodies in the house around the corner, Dogbite was anxious to distance himself from the murder scene.

"Yo, how the fuck these niggas just disappear?" Hotrod vented, still looking around in hopes of a miracle. "And 'Bite, I had them niggas, bro. I was on they ass for real. You seen that shit."

"Yeah, I hear you, bro." Dogbite nodded, thinking it was Mecca who Hotrod needed to plea his case to. "But right now, we need to move around. Cause them niggas in the wind."

Reluctantly telling Dogbite to pull off, Hotrod was definitely dreading the call to Mecca. She was a woman with a low tolerance for failure and excuses.

"Aye, I think the nigga busting at me was Double-O, too," Hotrod said as they rode back to the duck-off Mecca had provided. "And by Allah... I'm on that nigga ass 'til one of us dead!"

***

On the bottom floor of an east side apartment, Teer splashed gasoline over the walls and furniture. Having already saturated the upstairs, he hated to burn down a building that had brought in a quarter-million in its thirty-day span. But Asha was still insistent on switching locations, so like a good soldier he simply followed his orders.

At just 17-years-old, Teer could honestly claim that he had more money than the average adult. Subjected to stimulant fumes while in his mother's womb, he felt like he'd been fending for survival since he learned how to crawl. So, although it required him to risk his life and freedom on a daily basis, the loyalty he lent to Lo-Lo and the twins was well deserved; for they had unselfishly pulled him from the pool of poverty.

Leaving behind a flame-engulfed building, Teer calmly walked down the street and climbed into the Denali's backseat.

As Noni shifted the SUV into drive and drive off, she glanced at Teer through the rearview mirror. "Aye, me and Lo-Lo was just talking, right? And lil' nigga it dawned on us that you been stacking some serious paper. So, we wanna know, how much you got stuffed in your mattress?"

Teer smiled at their nosiness. "Noni, I love y'all to death, and I think you know that. But I'ma have to plead the fif' on that one, my baby."

Returning the smile, she bobbed her head in respect at his response. "A'ight, I can accept that. But you better not be spending all your money on these lil' fast-ass girls."

"Nah, never that. I be telling them to keep that same energy they had when I was stealing to eat, you feel me."

"Tell the truth, Teer," Lo-Lo said as they turned into a gas station. "You ain't never took your lil' mans for a swim, have you?"

He busted out laughing. "Man, y'all fooling! What type of question is that?"

"Just answer it," Noni insisted as she pulled up to a pump. "'Cause if you need some assistance, I can definitely find you a lot-lizard that'll lick that lil' thang to death. Have you balled up in fetal, sucking your thumb like a baby."

Teer was in tears, clutching his stomach from the pain of excessive laughter. Although Teer eluded their question, he had actually engaged in several solicited sexual affairs. But like a little brother would, he found it awkward to discuss his sex life with women he looked at like biological sisters.

After going inside to pay for the gas, Lo-Lo was on her way out, when she nearly collided with a well-dressed stranger who was dangerously handsome.

"Empty yo' pockets," he ordered, blocking her from going around.

Lo-Lo frowned up at him. "For what?"

"'Cause you damn near ran me the fuck over. So, you must've stole something and you trying to get away. Now show me what you took, so I can go in there and pay for it. 'Cause you too pretty to be out here stealing, you feel me."

"Boy, ain't nobody stole nothing." Lo-Lo laughed. "And it was your clumsy-ass that almost ran into me. Now watch out, before my girl think it's a problem over here."

He threw his hands up in surrender. "Aw, my fault. I ain't know you was on the LGBTQ-plus committee. I already know the pull y'all got, and I apologize. I don't want no smoke."

"If you don't stop playing with me." Lo-Lo playfully pushed him. "I'm strictly dickly, okay?"

He sized her up in a lustful manner. "Well, in that case, let the record reflect, if it ain't snowing I ain't going. Only thing I want black is my coffee, you hear me!"

As they joined in laughter, Lo-Lo approvingly assessed his appearance. Along with the stylish placement of a ballcap over his shoulder-length dreads, he flaunted a small fortune in the form of a yellow-gold Cuban with flickering stones.

"I'm Uno." He extended his hand, to which Lo-Lo shook it and told him her name. "A'ight, gimme your number and just one conversation," Uno urged her with a direct stare. "And if I can't keep you laughing the whole call, then I'll move to Nebraska and change my name to Norman."

Feeling and his vibe and vernacular, Lo-Lo was eyeing him in contemplation, when her thoughts were interrupted by the blaring of a horn. "Aye, I gotta go," she said upon noticing Noni waving her hand in urgency.

"I'm saying, what's up with your number?" he called out after her.

"If it's meant for you to have it, we'll meet back up," Lo-Lo said before hopping in the truck.

Impressed by a white girl he sensed to be different, Uno watched the SUV as it sped out the gas station. *I'ma see you around.*

"What the fuck was that all about?" Noni inquired, looking at Uno in the rearview.

Wearing the grin of a schoolgirl, Lo-Lo shrugged. "Just some boy I met. And if you hadn't been banging on the horn all crazy and shit, I might've got his number."

"Yeah, well, why you out here popping corn with strangers, our peoples in danger."

"Who?" Lo-Lo turned to her in concern.

"Double-O and CJ," Noni spat. "They out here trying put in work on our behalf, and you out here skinning and grinning with some corny-ass nigga."

"Noni, how was I supposed to know some shit was going on?" Lo-Lo defensively countered. "And soon as you hit the horn, didn't I come running?"

"If you was staying focused, you wouldn't have to be running."

"Oh, so Noni the only one who can have a sex life, huh?"

"Don't no emotions come with my shit."

"Are you being for real right now, Noni. Are you really gon' sit here and act like you ain't got no feelings for Angel?"

"Come on, you already know what the play was on that. And you was there when Asha put me on to her."

"Yeah, but that don't mean you ain't developed feelings. I see the way you be looking at her and shit."

With this being the first time Teer had witnessed the women bicker, he didn't know how or if he should defuse it.

But he knew if Asha was present, she'd dead the dispute with the clearing of her throat.

Their argument was paused as Noni turned down a west side street and sent Double-O a text. "Wya?"

Seconds after Noni sent it, Lo-Lo pointed to two figures creeping out of an old church. "There they go right there!"

As Noni sped up to them, Teer opened the back door and jumped in the third row.

"Got-damit man!" CJ sighed in relief as him and Double-O settled in the backseat. "That was some wild shit."

Before pulling off, Noni couldn't refrain from turning around to tease them, "A church though? You demonic-ass niggas hid in a church?"

CJ grinned. "Shit, when a nigga on yo' ass, you gotta think fast. And the same way you thinking is the same way we was hoping they was thinking. And you see we still here. So, Hallelujah, thank you, Jesus!"

"Oooh, y'all going to hell," Lo-Lo laughed as the truck rolled forward. "Do not pass 'go', do not collect 'two hundred dollars'. Straight to hell."

Double-O smirked. "I'd rather go to hell in the future, then a graveyard tonight."

While headed back to their side of town, Double-O explained that the sole reason they were still breathing was based on instinct. "'Cause if I ain't see him when I did, he would've turned us into t-shirts."

The truck grew quiet at the thought of how close they'd come to death. No matter who or how many a man may have killed, at any given moment his plug could be pulled in the same heartless manner.

"I'm saying, though," Noni broke the silence to ask a nagging question, "how the fuck did them niggas know where y'all was at?"

Assuming it was the same shooters from the liquor store incident, Double-O answered, "'Cause they been laying on us, that's how. We wasn't at the nigga, Smurf, house for ten minutes before that shit jumped off. So that means we out here lacking for real. And this the second time. And you know what they say about three strikes..."

At the chilling thought of being struck out, Lo-Lo couldn't help but peer at her side mirror and wonder if the truck was being currently followed.

Chapter 6

Clutching nine-pound rifles of forged steel and plywood—commonly known as AK-47's— a group of Dullah's demons were locked onto a canary yellow Porsche as it pulled inside the chop shop. Planted at the stop of the staircase was the monarch himself, whose face has half hidden behind a haze of cigar smoke.

With their safety switches disengaged, the demons eyed Asha's every move as she emerged from the driver seat; wearing a belted Burberry raincoat and oversized shades.

Upon scanning the Porsche's interior, one of the men gave Dullah an affirmative nod, a signal that Asha had come alone.

"Pat her down, Rome," Dullah ordered, exhaling a flow of fumes from his flared nostrils.

A weaponless Rome stepped forward to follow orders. "Ain't no hard feelings," he whispered to Asha while conducting the frisk.

After being assured Asha was unarmed, Dullah then instructed Rome to check the trunk of her car. Rome frowned in irritation at the man's paranoia before turning to Asha.

Without the slighted resistance, she fished the keys from her coat pocket and dropped them into Rome's extended hand.

Along with a pair of gunman, whose rifles were aimed at the rear enclosure, Rome approached the trunk and inserted the key. He glanced at Asha for a sign of impending danger, saw nothing suspicious, then held his breath and popped the trunk.

Exhaling in relief at sight of the empty enclosure, Rome slammed it shut and looked up at Dullah. "It's good, boss."

Dullah sucked on the cigar tip before beckoning Asha with a wave of the hand. "A'ight, come on up."

When she reached the top of the staircase and stood before him, Dullah was rewarded with the sweet-smelling fragrance of Chanel°5. Briefly succumbing to his lower desires, he allowed his gaze to travel from her pent-up hair to the delicate neck on which he'd love to nibble. "So, what's on your mind?" he brusquely inquired, as if his brain was centered on strictly business.

"Unless you get off on having an audience, then I suggest we talk inside your office."

Although the limb between his legs was aroused from its sleep, Dullah put a leash on his lust and squinted at Asha through skeptical eyes. "What kind of games you playing? 'Cause my name ain't Milton, and I don't know no Bradley."

"I'ma grown-ass woman, Dullah. Now if me coming here was a waste of our time, then I'll turn right around and march back down these stairs."

He studied her closely before stepping closer. When he held out his hand as if to touch her, he instead reached around to open the door to his office. "Ladies first."

Entering the room without hesitation, Asha removed her shades and posed before him in a wide-legged stance.

When Dullah followed her inside and closed the door, Asha maintained eye contact as she undid her coat and let it fall to the floor.

Unable to believe what he was seeing, Dullah was filled with a mixture of emotions - mainly surprise. This was an event he had envisioned for quite some time but had recently resolved would never take place.

"Is it how you thought it would look?" Asha asked, flaunting a flawless figure in lace undergarments and pointed-toe heels.

As if he was recording every inch of her skin to a disk in his memory, he studied her body with unblinking intensity. Of all the womanly shapes he had ever examined, Asha by far owned the most intriguing. But before fully submitting to his fleshly desires, he cautiously questioned, "Why the sudden change of heart?"

"Because like you once said, 'without the resources, aspirations are nothing more than farfetched dreams'. And we all know life is about position. So, if you getting on top of me will help me get on top of the world, then I think that's worth the value of my virginity. So, you gon' keep standing there, staring?" Asha put her hands on her waist in impatience, "or you gon' come get what we both know you want?"

Abandoning the cigar in an astray, he advanced toward her with a predatory glare. After years of yearning for her youthful uterus, he would finally crush her rebellion with his 8-inch club. When picking her up by her balloon-like bottom, Dullah fought for control as his fingers sunk into the satiny softness. *I'ma make her have blood and cum all over this dick*, he crudely thought to himself.

With her arms wrapped around his neck, Asha let out a hiss as his lips left kisses all over her chest. "Dullah, don't stop," she whined in his ear.

Without removing his mouth from her mango-flavored skin, he retreated to a couch and lowered himself onto it. Aside from being on a mission to maim her resistance, this was a long-awaited experience he would thoroughly enjoy.

"Aye, lift up real quick," he said, eager to expose his rock-hard erection. As he was unbuckling his jeans, Asha reached up and let down her hair.

Unaware of the icepick that suddenly appeared in her hand, Dullah's eyes bulged in shock as Asha buried the blade at the base of his skull. Due to the precision of her puncture, he was instantly reduced to a speechless paraplegic.

"Silly wabbit," Asha sang in a child-like tone. "How many times they tell you tricks are for kids? But don't worry," she consoled, rising from the couch to retrieve her coat. "I won't let you suffer too long." While Dullah glared through pools of hatred, she pulled up a chair and sat in front of him. "If the fish don't open its mouth, it can't get caught. Does that make sense to you, Dullah?" As the fire in his eyes burned brighter in response, Asha calmly continued, "Well, assuming it doesn't, it means you talk too fucking much. The last time we saw each other, you were basically saying I owed you for finding out the men who killed Regina and raped my sister. But the thing is, me and Noni never told nobody about what happened to her. Not even Lo-Lo. So, for you to know could only mean one thing..."

Knowing he was living on borrowed time, if Dullah could talk, he'd gladly reveal how much he had paid for the sexual assault. How he found considerable joy from the shackles of trauma that pledged to keep Noni imprisoned in pain. Or how his death wouldn't deter Mecca and Unique from seeking revenge.

"Look at you." Asha scoffed in contempt. "A pitiful image of a man. Which is why you gon' die all alone with your shriveled-up dick out. And contrary to what I'm sure you believed, you was never cut out to be a true King." After a moment of returning his stare with even greater hatred, Asha patted his knee and rose to her feet. "Well, I guess I better get going. So, I'll leave you alone with whatever evil thoughts that brainless head is thinking. You know, being as though that's all you got left."

Upon her reaching around to slowly extract the blade from his skull, a stream of blood began flowing from the hole. Asha wiped off the blade on his shirt sleeve, then gathered her hair and used the icepick to pin it back up.

Pausing at the door, she turned to face Dullah and waved in farewell. "Oh, and by the way." She smiled. "Noni sends her regards."

Rome included, all eyes were on Asha as she came out the office descended the staircase. She licked her lips and lewdly disclosed, "That's how you put a nigga to sleep without making a sound."

Several men grabbed their crotch and groaned in desire, having no idea that her statement was literal.

As Asha awakened the Porsche with the touch of a button, Rome stepped forward to offer an apology. "It was never personal."

Bobbing her head in understanding as she slid behind the wheel, Asha replied before reversing out the garage, "And neither is this."

Once the nose of the car had cleared the building's threshold, Asha stepped on the brakes. Then, in response to Rome's puzzled expression, she reached beneath the seat and retrieved a green hand grenade. This was what she'd secretly purchased from Reverend Daniels.

As the garage door was mechanically lowering, Asha pulled the pin out the grenade and tossed it inside the shop. With no way of escaping as the door fully closed, she could imagine the men senselessly scattering for safety.

Replacing her shades as she sped out the scrapyard, Asha flinched at the sound of the loud explosion. With her nemesis and his minions blown into pieces, she could now focus her attention squarely on the construction of an empire.

Asha had patiently listened to everyone's thoughts on how they believed the situation should be handled. And while she valued their opinions, this was an instance that required her to make an executive decision. Because what was the sense in cutting off limbs, when you could save yourself time and go straight for the head.

Chapter 7

"These bitches babies!" Mecca quietly fumed in frustration, as her and Unique sat on a bench at a dog park. "And it's way past their bedtime."

From Smurf's failure to Hotrod's fumble and Dullah's demise, the twins were becoming a migraine to Mecca. But with her being a firm believer that cooler heads prevailed, she knew the importance of controlling her emotions. She just had to be patient; because a dog that ran fast didn't run long.

At the thought of a dog, Mecca's own canine, Mister, came over to lay his head on her lap. "You tired, boy?" She rubbed his fawn-colored head in affection. "All them other dogs done wore you out?"

Originally named Squeeze, Mister was a one-eyed pit-bull that once belonged to the incarcerated Kavoni. But after the gruesome discovery of the animal being involved with dog fighting, Mecca had decided that along with taking Kavoni's freedom and fortune, she'd also include the dog.

With Mister on a leash, Mecca and Unique leisurely strolled through the park. While staring straight ahead, Unique spoken from the heart, "We've accomplished a whole lot, sis. We both know our struggle. And as much as I miss Pee-Wee and Otha, I don't wanna just throw everything away for two people we can't bring back. I ain't suggesting we let it slide, but I think we gotta be careful on how we deal with this one."

"I hear you, Ni-Ni," Mecca replied. "And I can't say I don't understand where you coming from. But these are two lil' girls who still got Similac on their breath. And you know my work. You seen how I dismantled Kavoni's whole operation."

"Yeah, and that was when we had nothing to lose and everything to gain," Unique pointed out. "And I gotta keep it a buck, cuz and them was family, but Amiri was our heart. Come on, Mecca, you know that was a whole different fuel. But like I said, we ain't ducking nothing. But like you taught me, what's the easiest way to pass a test?"

Inwardly pleased by her sister's recollection, Mecca answered with a smile, "By doing your homework."

"Exactly. Which is what we haven't done. Which is likely why our problem still ain't solved. So, let's get back to the basics and nip this shit in the bud."

As they walked back to the car, Mecca glanced at Unique with a peculiar look.

"What?" Unique curiously smiled.

"Nah, it's just, I'm usually the one dishing out counsel on self-control. So to have you giving me a straightener is a beautiful thing. Cause it means you've been listening. And I'm proud of you, girl."

Touched by the sincerity of Mecca's statement, Unique stopped walking and embraced her sister. "Thank you, Mecca, I really needed to hear that. And don't ever forget, without you in my life, I'd probably be somewhere lost right now."

Adoptive sisters, Mecca and Unique had been joined at the hip since middle school. When Unique was being bounced from one foster home to another - where she often the victim of sexual abuse, it was Mecca who convinced her mother to legally bring her best friend into their close-knit clan. And when Unique had been teased by boys in school about her dark complexion and short, coarse hair, it was Mecca who stood her before a mirror and convinced her she was pretty. And in return for love she knew to be genuine, Unique signed her life over to loyalty and gave ownership to Mecca.

Approaching the Mercedes Benz wagon, Mecca opened the back door and Mister leaped inside. While he normally liked to stare out the window as he rode in traffic, the dog laid down on the seat in exhaustion.

"As much as I hate to admit it." Unique smirked as Mecca drove out the park. "Don't these two lil' girls kind of remind you of somebody?"

Mecca grinned, for she had secretly entertained the same thought. "Yeah, they do. And under different circumstances, I'd consider taking them under our wing. Cause they definitely got potential."

Unique added, "And ain't no denying they definitely dangerous."

Not far from the park, Mecca turned into the lot of a senior living resort. Although this trip came with emotional grief, they faithfully showed up on a weekly basis.

"We been coming here what, like three years now?" Unique stared toward the building. "And you would think it would easier, but it don't. It's like it hurt a little more each time."

Mecca didn't immediately respond, but she made it make sense when she did. "I feel your pain, trust me. But this ain't about us, Ni-Ni. So, we gotta stay strong for someone who once stood strong for us. Now put your game face on, and let's go play our position with positive vibes."

With Mister in tow, Mecca and Unique held hands as they entered the building's front lobby. As usual, they were warmly greeted by a senior employee who sat behind the desk.

"Oh, look at my two favorite young ladies!" The woman beamed. "I know Ms. Turner will be so happy to see you."

Upon reaching a door at the end of a hallway, Mecca inhaled a deep breath before turning its knob.

Despite entering the room with comforting smiles; as it happened every time, their hearts broke into pieces at the sight of their bedridden mother.

Chapter 8

Inside a downtown building that was currently undergoing renovation, Asha had a diagram spread out over a table as she barked commands at the crew of construction workers. Wearing a hardhat over her braided ponytail, she sported a pair of pink Timb's and gray coveralls.

"And I want this wall right here knocked down!" She tapped the diagram with her highlighter. "My goal is to add more space to this room."

After receiving a phone call from the bank manager, informing her of the loan being approved, an ecstatic Asha had immediately reached out to the former owner of the building in which she presently stood. Forced to shut down his club after a deadly shooting inside the men's bathroom, he agreed to part ways with the deed for $150,000. But of course, Asha convinced him it would be in his best 'profitable' interest to accept the payment in product.

Once a deal was struck and exchanges were made, she then had D'Aura file with department of commerce for a liquor license. Needless to say, the Butterfly Mafia were officially legitimate business owners.

Amid the clamor of drills and sledgehammers, Asha felt her phone vibrating in her back pocket and took the call through her AirPod.

After a brief conversation, she told the caller to pull around back upon their arrival. "And I'll meet you out there."

As Asha passed by the bar, she stopped to address D'Aura, who was in charge of its remodeling. "How's it going, love?"

She smiled. "It's gon' be a beautiful set up, Asha. From the floors to the height of the barstools. And I'ma do a Caesarstone bar top. So, it won't bulge or get wet from the drinks."

Before soon excusing herself, Asha listened with pleasure as D'Aura excitedly rambled on about all the upgrades. The girl was genuinely happy, which was an infectious feeling with someone like Asha.

Not long after Asha stepped out the back door did a dump truck come rumbling around the building and squeak to a stop. In hardhats and bright apparel, Double-O and CJ hopped down from the truck.

As they informed Asha that everything had gone well, a van with 'Cornerstone Ministries' stencilled on its door panels pulled up and parked behind the dump truck. Behind the van's wheel was Lo-Lo, who was clad in a black-and-white habit often worn by Nuns.

CJ climbed onto the back of the dump truck and hurled himself over into its dirt-filled bed. Seconds after sifting through a certain section of the soil, he uncovered a duffel bag and tossed it over to Double-O.

Courtesy of Lo-Lo, this was the ingenious method in which they'd haul their drug shipments upon pickup. And the church van was Asha's idea, as she had built a business relationship with Reverend Daniels.

After the drugs were stashed in back of the van, Lo-Lo winked at Asha before driving off. Although the quantity of drugs being conveyed carried a double-digit prison sentence, all parties present were certain she'd be safe, herself included. For what cop would think to pull over a church van, especially one being driven by a white woman wearing a habit.

As Lo-Lo drove out the parking lot and merged back into traffic, the Denali soon followed suit. With Angel driving and Noni riding shotgun, Teer sat behind them with a Draco on his lap.

"Lo-Lo looking like the real deal," Angel jokingly commented, trailing the van at a discreet distance.

"Can you please be quiet right now?" Noni sternly replied.

Angel frowned. "Be quiet for what?"

"'Cause right now ain't the time be talking. So, let's just stay on point and we can socialize later."

Biting back a sharp reply, Angel was thinking about the recent change in Noni's energy. She didn't know where or what it stemmed from, but what she did know was that she didn't like it one bit. And when they were finished 'staying on point', she intended to get to bottom of it.

Back at the building downtown, Asha was engaged in an earnest conversation with one of the construction crew members. She was explaining the importance of their work being completed by a certain date. And in return for accomplishing what would surely be an exhaustive feat, she promised to reward him and his crew with a handsome bonus.

He considered his men for a thoughtful moment, then, deciding they had what it took to pull it off, he extended his hand and said that she had a deal.

When noticing that D'Aura was waving for her attention, Asha quickly excused herself and hurried over to the bar. "Is everything good?" she asked as D'Aura was slipping on her jacket.

"That's the problem." D'Aura laughed, reaching for her purse. "It's going too damn good. Girl, how come I almost forgot I gotta pick my baby up from daycare. Fucking with you, they gon' have children services all over my ass!"

Apologizing for not being more mindful of the time, Asha escorted D'Aura out to her car, where they quickly hugged before she hopped in the Nissan and sped off.

After watching the car until it was no longer visible, Asha turned to proudly examine her new establishment. She allowed herself a subtle smile, for she was an actual business owner before the age of twenty-one.

On her way back inside, Asha noticed an area of the building where the paint was peeling. Glad that she'd saw it, it was a reminder for her to reach out to a painting company. There was nothing wrong with the building being beige, but she had a color scheme in mind that would better suit what she had in store.

"The city ain't gon' be ready for this." She smiled to herself before reentering the building.

Following Dullah's death, it felt to Asha like a looming dark cloud was no longer above her. Noni had voiced her disapproval over not being included, but Asha had wisely explained that the means of his demise was a one-woman job. With a burden behind her and success in her sights, Asha was ready to embrace life on a much grander scale.

But first, there was one more move to be made before she officially closed the book of Dullah.

Chapter 9

"If we locked in ain't no switching up/ Brodie came home, went to pick him up/ stolen Trackhawk got it tinted up/ caught him outside now he in a blunt/ ain't no falling off, I done put two million up..."

As Detroit natives Peezy and several other rap artists boastfully barked over an infectious beat, CJ, Double-O and Noni were weaving through traffic in a Trackhawk. End route to an auto body shop that specialized in restoration and custom paint jobs, Noni was anxious to see the GTO's makeover.

With the incident at the liquor store leaving a pair of bullet holes near the GTO's rear bumper, Noni had dropped the car off at the shop, along with eighty-five grand. Her only request to the owner was that he return a toy that would be the talk of the city; even if it meant forking over extra fees.

"Noni, you back there geeking like shit!" CJ teased from behind the wheel.

"Hell yeah, nigga!" She grazed her palms together in anticipation. "He say my shit finna make 'em hate!"

For $85,000, the owner had moved Noni's car to the front of the line. He worked long hours, expedited orders, and applied certain touches that were guaranteed to please her. He had called her this morning to inform her that her toy was ready.

They were flying down Six Mile, when Noni leaned forward and gripped the side of CJ's seat. "Aye, turn around real quick."

"Turn around for what?"

Even Double-O was curious to hear her response.

"'Cause I need to make a stop," she said, looking over her shoulder. "I just thought about it when we passed that plaza back there. Now turn this mu'fucka around and quit asking questions, nigga." They were soon parking in front of a house Noni pointed out. "This ain't gon' take long, so keep this bitch running."

"Noni, can I come with you?" Double-O asked as she halfway out the car.

Touched by the concern in his tone, she paused and smiled. "Nah, my baby, you good. This ain't even that type of party."

Thinking of Double-O in fondness as she mounted the front porch, Noni raised her hand to knock, thought better of it and rang the doorbell instead.

The door opened a minute later and a familiar face came into view. "Hi, Ms. Johnson." Noni smiled.

"Well, would you look—" The elderly lady stared in surprise. Then she narrowed her eyes and seriously inquired. "You ain't running from them po-lice again now, is you?"

"No, ma'am." Noni laughed. "I just wanted to stop by and say thank you again for what you did."

Ms. Johnson turned to scold the Rottweiler, Missy, who had grown antsy with excitement over Noni's scent. "Girl, would you calm down. You only met her once."

"She good judge of character," Noni offered on the dog's behalf.

"Yeah, well, you must be something, for her to have let you get in her doghouse like that."

Ms. Johnson then looked past Noni and nosily asked, "Chile, how you get over her? Your sister bring you?"

To prevent the woman's view of Double-O and CJ, Noni shifted and aimlessly aimed at her thumb toward the street. "I'm in that green car over there."

Ms. Johnson squinted for a closer look, then gave up with a grunt and opened the door. "Well, you might as well come on in, 'cause it don't seem like Missy gon' have it no other way."

Conscious of the time, and the fact that she'd told her friends to keep the car running, Noni hesitated a split second before stepping inside. Double-O and CJ would just have to sit tight.

With her backend wagging furiously, Missy was overly anxious for Noni's affection. "Hey, lil' mama!" she sang to the dog, ruffling her fur with both hands. "You miss me, huh?"

Closing and locking the front door, Ms. Johnson observed their playful interaction before walking towards the back of the house. "I've had Missy since she was just a baby," the woman said while tinkering around in what sounded like the kitchen, "and I've never seen her behave that with other family members, let alone a stranger."

Noni was sending Double-O a quick text when Ms. Johnson returned from the kitchen with a tray of homemade cookies and two glasses of milk.

"Chile, you gotta excuse my manners," the woman apologized upon catching her texting. "'Cause I'm probably holding you up, ain't I?"

Noni shook her head and lied with a straight face. "No, ma'am."

From the house being ghostly quiet, to the chocolate-chip-entrapment, it was obvious the lady was lonely; and Noni didn't have the heart to ruin her moment. The car and her cronies could wait.

"I just baked these this morning," Ms. Johnson said, taking a seat next to Noni on the sofa. "I gotta grandbaby that stop by from time to time. And when he do, he always looking for something sweet. He think his grandmama don't know he be smoking that reefa."

Noni laughed. "Ms. Johnson, what you know about some reefa?"

She huffed. "I wasn't always a God-fearing woman, now. I've done my fair share of sinning. But then the good Lord showed me the error in my ways."

When Noni reached for a cookie, Missy instantly went into a seated position and eyed her intensely. She wanted a cookie, too. And she felt it was the least Noni could do after using her doghouse as a hideout.

Noni looked to Ms. Johnson for approval, who gave her consent with a stern finger. "She get just one, and that's all."

Missy scarfed down the cookie, licked her chops once and pinned Noni with a pleading expression. If she could just have one more.

As Ms. Johnson was on the verge of telling Missy 'no', Noni grabbed another cookie and accidentally dropped it. "Oh, damn!" she said as Missy quickly made it disappear. Then she looked at Ms. Johnson and apologized. "Excuse my language, I'm sorry."

Ms. Johnson looked from Noni to Missy. "You dropped it on purpose, didn't you?" she accused Noni.

Grinning in guilt, Noni held up her hands. "Sometimes I can be clumsy. So don't blame Missy for taking advantage."

"See, y'all think y'all slick." Ms. Johnson wagged her finger. "But you know what?" She pointed to a blanket over in the corner. "Missy, go lay down. And I'ma deal with you later. And see how it long it be before you get another treat."

Missy moped over to her makeshift bed and flopped down. But she positioned herself to where she could stare at Noni through saddened eyes.

"Don't look at her," Ms. Johnson advised. "That's how she try to get what she wants. By looking all pitiful and stuff. She can't stand to be told 'no'."

"That's the same thing my sister say about me." Noni smiled.

"How is your sister, by the way? I remember how worried you had her."

"She good. She trying to start some type of business that she keeping a secret right now. So, she acting like she super busy. But other than that, she doing good."

"And your parents? How are they?"

"Well, we ain't never met our father. And Regina got killed like four years ago."

"And I'm assuming Regina was your mother?"

Noni nodded.

"I'm so sorry to hear that." She took Noni's hands in consolation. "I know it must be hard for you and your sister to be without either parent. Y'all both just babies."

"It's what was given to us." Noni shrugged. "But long as I got my twin, I'm good."

"So, you two are identical?"

Noni shook her head. "Fraternal."

"And did your mother ever say how she came up with the names, Asha and Noni?"

"Yeah, she said they Swahili. I guess they told her she was gon' have a difficult pregnancy, and that one of us might not make it. So, Regina said that when my sister came out first, she was Asha, which means 'Life' in Swahili. And when I came, I was Noni, which means a 'A Gift of God'."

"Oh, that's so precious!" Ms. Johnson squeezed her hand. "But let me ask you something. Why do you refer to your mother by her name?"

Noni looked down and the woman implored, "What is it, Noni?"

Without looking up, Noni answered, "Because a mother is someone who loves and protects her child. So, to me, Regina a woman who don't deserve that title."

Ms. Johnson groaned in sorrow at the weight of her statement. "And does your sister know how you feel?"

Noni nodded.

From life experience and common sense, Ms. Johnson knew that the emotional void between the mother and daughter was likely a result of Noni's sexual orientation. Her mother had endured a troubled pregnancy, only to later discover that one of her twin girls identified with the opposite sex. In her disappointment, and likely shame-filled state, she had allowed herself to favor one child over the other; not knowing the internal damage being caused to her other imperfect child. Guilty of once making a similar mistake, Ms. Johnson personally knew the aftereffects of a child who felt unloved.

"Noni, look at me."

When Noni looked up, Ms. Johnson felt genuine pain at the sight of Noni's teary eyes. *You poor baby*, she sadly thought to herself.

"I'll never know everything you've been through, and I don't expect you to tell me," Ms. Johnson spoke from her heart. "But what I do know is that the most important love we can receive comes from above. And I know you might think, 'well, if He loved me, why would He let me go through what all I've been through'. And the answer is because we were all given free-will, your mother included. But regardless of what she did to make you feel unloved, you're still standing. So don't let the pain from your past prevent you from having a fruitful future. Cause then every battle you've fought and won will have been in vain. Do you understand me, girl?"

Noni bobbed her head, wondering if her life would've been different with the presence of a loving grandmother.

"Now, I'm not gon' sit here and preach every book of the Bible to you," Ms. Johnson continued, "but before you go, I would like to say a prayer over you. That's only if you don't mind or won't feel uncomfortable."

Although she had never felt a connection with her creator, Noni consented out of respect for her elder.

Scooting closer, Ms. Johnson bowed her head, prompting Noni to follow suit. The woman then earnestly prayed, "My dear Heavenly Father, I humbly come before you as a sinful servant in search of your undeserved services. You are a merciful God, the embodiment of love, which is why You don't force us to follow You. But Lord, it says in your Word, the Holy Bible, that there is more joy in Heaven over one repentant sinner then ninety-nine faithful followers. So, I'm asking that You lay a healing hand over this young lady's heart and revive it with the desire to reroute her journey in a more joyful direction. Help her decipher the difference between believing and belonging. Because to belong to You is to receive eternal life, something no earthly being could ever provide..."

As Noni gave ear to the poetic flow of the heartfelt entreaty, she felt the woman's passion through the occasional squeezing of her hands. This was someone who was solid in their Godly beliefs.

When the prayer was eventually brought to a close, Noni was surprised to herself say, "Amen."

"Faith without works is frivolous," Ms. Johnson counseled Noni as she walked her to the front door. "I don't doubt you've had hard parts in your life, but, Noni, you're now of age to where you gotta take accountability for your actions. We can only use our past as a crutch for so long, before it becomes an unpleasant tune to the ears of our Lord."

"I hear you, ma'am. And I ain't gon' sit here and say I'ma wake up tomorrow a Born-Again Christian, but I promise to keep in mind everything you've told me. And I appreciate the prayer, it was beautiful. I wish I would've had somebody like you in my life a long time ago."

"Chile, it ain't never too late for some good old fashion motherly love. So, make sure you don't be no stranger around here. You can come see me and Missy whenever you want. And bring Asha next time."

Assuring her she would, Noni withdrew a bundle of bills from her britches and held them out for Ms. Johnson to take. "This the least I can do after you saving my life."

She laid a hand over Noni's and politely declined. "I'm touched by the gesture, but I can't accept that. And believe me, my Heavenly Father takes real good care of me."

After hugging Ms. Johnson and bending to pet Missy, Noni promised to soon return and turned to leave.

"Hey, Noni!" Ms. Johnson called through the screen door. When Noni paused on the porch, Ms. Johnson made a statement that would linger in Noni's mind for days to come. "If you should soon find yourself stuck in an undesirable situation, instead of complaining, see it as a sign of affection. Because it says in the Bible that God 'disciplines those He loves'."

As Noni reentered the Jeep, CJ had his lips fixed to fire off joke. But upon noticing the serious look on her face, he replaced the joke with a sincere inquiry, "Wassup, you good?"

She nodded, staring out her window in deep thought. Because if what the woman said was true, Noni just hoped the discipline didn't involve the separation from her sister.

They were back in traffic when Double-O wordlessly passed Noni his phone. It showed a news report of two dead bodies being recently discovered inside a west side home. With plastic bags placed over their heads, the two suffocated men were Pierre and Smurf.

"That's how they knew where me and CJ was at that night," Double-O said. "'Cause they had already killed them niggas, and was waiting on us to show up. So Dullah might be gone, but I need to know if whoever thought to do some shit like that still alive. 'Cause if so, they some vicious-ass dogs that need to be put down, immediately!"

Chapter 10

Wayne State

Asha was headed to her next class, when the boy, Jaylen, hurried to catch up to her. "Hey, what's going on? I haven't really being seeing you since the semester changed. How you been doing?"

"I've been doing alright, and you?"

He shrugged. "You know, still staying optimistic and waiting on that phone call. Hoping you'll eventually decide to give a square a shot."

Asha smiled, to which he jokingly added, "But I'm saying, if my approach is wrong, just let me know. Cause for you, I'm willing to get on some gangsta shit. I can go get tatted up, and start throwing up gang signs in this bitch."

Asha laughed as she imagined him going from a pretty-boy to a Peezy.

"But seriously, though, Asha." He stopped walking. "I really like you. And I think you're very pretty. I know I might not fit the image of what or who you're normally attracted to, but don't a good heart count for something?"

"Jaylen, it has nothing to do with your image. And contrary to what you might think, I'm not even into street dudes like that. But like I told you before, I'm just not at a place in my life where I can afford an emotional attachment to anyone outside of family."

"Yeah, but I'm not asking you to get emotionally attached. I just wanna be friends. I'm so curious about you. And I got some many questions I wanna ask you."

"That's how every relationship starts, Jaylen— as friends. 'Cause sometimes feelings can be like wildfire and spread out of a person's control. But if it's any consolation..." She reached in her purse and pulled out a small piece of paper. "I still got your number."

Jaylen couldn't refrain from smiling at the sight of what he'd given her months ago. Maybe there was hope after all.

He called her name as she was on the verge of entering her next class. And when she turned, he smiled. "I like your new hairstyle. I think it really fits you."

Returning the smile as she reached up to touch her honey-colored twist-outs, Asha thanked him for the compliment and waved in goodbye.

As she sat in class, hardly hearing a word of what the professor was saying, Asha was thinking about her attraction to Jaylen. The boy was handsome, hilarious, and harbored an aura of honesty. Unbeknownst to him, he fit the image of what she had envisioned in her teenage fantasies. But for reasons she couldn't disclose, she couldn't allow him access inside her world. And it wasn't as if she was opposed to the idea, but it was more of a mental barrier she didn't know how to break down.

Without the courage to confide in even her closest friends, Asha had come to the sad conclusion that falling in love was not something she would ever experience.

Chapter 11

With the city under siege by the overhead sun, Belle Isle Island was packed. As usual, there were a number of illegal activities in motion.

As a crowd were noisily huddled around a high-stakes dice game, heads began swiveling towards a three-car motorcade that entered the park. While this was nothing uncommon, it was the lead vehicle that kidnapped their attention.

Bearing a white, Gucci top over a candy-pink paint job, the sparkling GTO sat on 26-inch Forgi's with pink lipstick. As the toy-looking coup came to a stop in the center of the park, the Gucci top began to slowly retract; revealing the faces of three hooded females who were vibing to a song by Nicki Minaj.

"...Until I'm at the pearly white gates I gotta move something, do something/ all meetings happen in person, so they can't prove nothing/ tryna run the country one day like Putin, but who's rushing? who's bluffing?"

Protectively parked behind the GTO were two towering F-150 Super Crews. Powder-blue over chrome wheels and matching pipes, the 'Black Widow' editions were valued at nearly $100,000.

The doors of both pickups simultaneously opened and out stepped Double-O, CJ, and six other stone-faced felons. As if they were licensed to carry citizens, several of the men had tactical weapons wedged in their visible holsters.

Amid a chattering crowd of inquisitive onlookers, Asha, Lo-Lo and Noni emerged from the GTO in pink hoodies.

"That's them Butterfly Mafia bitches!" a nearby woman informed her friend. "I heard them hoes think they super turnt. Especially the one with the plaits."

Her friend smacked her lips. "Bruh, I'll beat one of them hoes up for real. They out here with that whack-ass white bitch. Fuck they do that at?"

While the two vipers continued to spit venom on women they'd never even met, Double-O and CJ unrolled the bedcover on their truck and uncovered several large trash bags. They looked at each other and grinned, for they were about to ignite a full fledge frenzy.

Untying the bags, which were filled with small baggies of light-green buds, they reached in to grab handfuls and began passing them out to the crowd. It wasn't long before a stampede ensued, as the word of 'free weed' quickly spread through the park.

Among the herd were two venomous women, who both wore wide grins as their outstretched hands were awarded 3.5's of an exotic strand.

The cannabis clearance came courtesy of Dullah, who Asha was certain was turning in his grave. After his literal disintegration, she had directed Double-O and his rebels to raid every weed house belonging to Dullah.

Although it was likely today's giveaway would elicit suspicion in regard to their involvement with Dullah's dethronement, Asha had decided the notorious notion was worthy of being attributed to the Butterfly Mafia.

A group of admirers were assembled around Noni as she took them on a tour of her new toy. With the doors left open, some used their phones to record the interior. There were ostrich seats that had Butterfly outlines stitched in the head rests. A detachable pink-and-white Forgiato steering wheel, and an 8-inch screen on the dash that listed a number of functions.

Observing Noni with a subtle smile, Asha was filled with genuine joy at the sight of her sister's excitement. She loved that girl to a fearful degree, as a parent would their own precious child.

"Girl, what you so deep in thought about over here?" Lo-Lo smiled, appearing at Asha's side.

She nudged her head at Noni. "Look at my lil' baby, Lo'. Look at how happy she is over that car."

Lo-Lo nodded in agreement. "Yeah, she definitely ain't stopped smiling since she picked it up."

Asha turned to Lo-Lo and declared, "I love that girl like I gave birth to her myself, Loretta. And I can't even explain the fear I feel when I think about something happening to her."

Lo-Lo laid a hand of comfort on Asha's arm. "Noni might get a lil' reckless sometimes, but she ain't—"

"Lo-Lo, don't do that," Asha cut her off with a firm head shake. "Don't try to downplay the danger that come with doing dirt. 'Cause regardless of our cause, we just as susceptible to death as anybody else out here in these streets. We don't get no pass just 'cause of our past, and you know that."

"So, what you suggesting? 'Cause it seems you clearly been giving this some thought."

"I'm suggesting I figure out how to stop being a hypocrite. Because it's like, how can I say I love either of y'all, or myself, if I'm endangering our lives on a daily basis? You don't put the people you love in harm's way; you do everything you can to protect them."

"But you have been protecting us, Asha. Shit, everything we got is basically because of you. I understand where you coming from, but you shouldn't be so hard on yourself. You one helluva of a woman, love. And even though we the same age, I truly admire you."

Appreciative of Lo-Lo's endearing statement, Asha gave her hug and flashed a mischievous grin. "I got something to show you."

"What?" Lo-Lo lit up.

But before Asha could could answer, someone tapped Lo-Lo on the shoulder and stole her attention.

"What up doe?" Uno greeted, smiling at Lo-Lo's surprised reaction. "I see you look just as good in the daytime as you do in the dark," he added in reference to their gas station encounter.

Lo-Lo reached for an imaginary walkie talkie on her hoodie and radioed for backup. "Security, we gotta stalker in the park. He kind of tall, with long dreads, and appear to be wearing a knockoff Polo jacket."

Uno chuckled at her sense of humor. "A'ight, I see you got jokes. That's wassup. Wanna try to clown me in front of your peoples."

After the two exchanged a handshake and flirtatious smiles, Lo-Lo introduced him to her peoples. "This my sister, Asha. And Asha, this Uno. The boy who been damn ran me over at the gas station."

Uno extended his hand to Asha. "How you doing?"

Removing a hand from her hoodie, she opted for a fist-bump. "I'm good. You?" Beneath his handsome features and costly fabrics, Asha detected the scent of a savage.

"Wassup, twin?" Noni walked up, assessing Uno with a shrewd once-over. "You Good?"

Lo-Lo lowered her head and shook it, for she just knew Noni was about to run the boy off.

"Yeah, we good," Asha assured her overprotective sister. "Lo-Lo was just introducing me to her friend, Uno."

"Uno?" she repeated, searching her brain for remembrance of the name. Then it dawned on her. "You that Bandgang nigga that be rapping?"

Confirming he was, he added with a grin, "And I bet you the one that was banging all over the horn at the gas station that night, too."

While Lo-Lo and Asha did their best to smother their smiles, an unamused Noni stepped closer to Uno and glared in his eyes. "I'm hip to you lil' rapper niggas. Y'all like to pass pussy around like it's a blunt. But I'm warning you right now, *Uno*, this a white girl I'm willing to die about. So, if in your little horny-ass mind you right think shit finna be sweet with her, then you might as well start looking around this parking lot for something different to fuck with."

As evidence she stood on every syllable of her sermon, Noni threw up the four fingers of her left hand. "Nigga, and that's on all Fo' of 'em."

Without a fraction of fear on his face, despite having heard of her murderous rep', Uno calmly replied, "You don't know me for real, so I can't even be offended. But I encourage you to ask around about me. 'Cause my name attached to the *utmost* respect."

Satisfied with his response, Asha told Uno it was nice meeting him, then took Noni by the hand and led her off. "Come on, love, let's let them talk for a minute."

Once they were alone, Lo-Lo informed him, "My sister super overprotective, so you gotta excuse her."

"And that's understandable. But like I said, I can stand a background check. My shit been A-one since day-one, you feel me?"

Lo-Lo playfully pushed him. "Why you ain't tell me you be rapping? Got me all in the dark and shit."

"'Cause a nigga gotta stay humble, you hear me? And besides, I ain't even made it yet. Outside of the D, don't nobody know who I am."

"Let me hear something." Lo-Lo smiled.

"Let you hear something?"

"Yeah, silly, spit something. And I'ma tell you if you got it or not."

With the confidence and ease of a veteran, Uno rapped, "Watch yo' peeps and play for keeps, cause kinfolk be the ones to leak/ now tryna get the window-seat with shackles on your wrists and feet/ on that rack with twenty-three, boy that ain't the road to go/ instead of being content with shit, the greed will make us go for mo'/ and bet you lose your hoe for sho', cause patience ain't her strong suit/ now you stressing in a cell no bigger than a phone booth/ slip and make the wrong move, DRC will own you/ and that crew you belong to, watch how they disown you..."

Lo-Lo's eyebrows rose in surprise. She was genuinely impressed by the delivery of his insightful lyrics. "Damn, that was nice. Like, to be honest, I didn't expect it to be that good. Yeah, if you stay at it, I guarantee you won't be local for long."

"Listen at you." Uno grabbed her by the hoodie and hauled her closer. "Trying to secure your spot already."

They happened to look to their left, where Asha and Noni were monitoring their movements from inside the car.

"Aye, listen, it was good seeing you, but I gotta go," Lo-Lo said in regret. "My sisters waiting on me."

"So, you not a woman of your word?"

"Of course, I am." Lo-Lo frowned.

"Remember last time I saw you, I asked for your number. You shot me dead and said if it was meant for me to have it I'd see you again. And here I am."

She eyed him with a subtle grin, recalling the statement she had definitely made. "How about you give me yours and I promise to call?"

"How 'bout we do the exchange, and I'll let you call first?"

Lo-Lo shrugged in confusion. "But what sense does that make? Waiting is waiting."

"'Cause if I feel you taking too long, I'ma call your ass first!"

Lo-Lo laughed before finally giving in. "Alright, but I'm telling you now, if you jump the gun, I'm not only gon' block you, but I'ma go downtown and put a restraining order on your ass."

As Uno was watching the two F-150's trail the hot-pink Pontiac out the park, one of his Bandgang members came to stand alongside him. "You know who them hoes is, don't you?"

Uno nodded, irritated by the unwanted intrusion.

"Them bitches plugged, my baby," his comrade continued in a conspiring tone. "So, if you can knock off that white bitch, we can take them hoes straight to the cleaners. Cause I hear they gotta building doing damn near ten-bands a day!"

Although this was all information of which Uno was already aware, setting up Lo-Lo was the furthest thing from his mind. Between loyalty to his clan and a longing for love, Uno was searching for a solution on how to balance the two. He just hoped it didn't come to the point where he was forced to make a choice. For the man standing beside him was his own flesh and blood.

Chapter 12

Alone in a bright red Nissan GT3, Double-O sped through traffic while conversing with Reverend Daniels via Bluetooth. On the passenger seat beside him was a Nike gym bag, with a loaded firearm lying on top.

"I'm headed your way now, Rev'," Double-O informed as he switched lanes. "And I got the full amount with me."

"Your integrity is admirable, little brother, but I've already taken care of it. If additional fees are required, I'll let you know. And I'll also be sure to share with our friend your willingness to contribute, as I'm sure it'll brighten his day."

Upon disconnecting the call, Double-O eyed his rearview before making a U-turn and punching the gas.

Reaching the outskirts of the city, he pulled into the parking lot of a prestigious law firm and double parked. Concealing the gun beneath his jacket, he grabbed the gym bag and hopped out.

Inside the expensively furnished establishment, Double-O was greeted by a female receptionist of foreign descent. "Good afternoon, sir, how may I help you?"

He sat the bag on the counter. "I'm here to see Mr. Shottenstein."

She glanced at the bag before making a brief phone call. Bearing a smile as she replaced the receiver, she informed Double-O he'd be met with in a moment.

A moment was more like twenty minutes. "Marty Shottenstein," greeted a gray-haired man of average height.

"I'm Marjuan," Double-O gripped his hand in a firm shake. "And I'm here on behalf of my friend, Kavoni McClain."

Led to an office that was befitting of a legendary appeal lawyer, Double-O was instructed to have a seat, to which he declined. "I'm just here to drop off the money for Kavoni's appeal."

Driven by greed but composed of character, the lawyer informed him that the fee had already been paid in its entirety.

"Yeah, I know." Double-O nodded, placing the bag on a chair and unzipping it. He removed loaves of bread, which he stacked on the lawyer's large oak desk. "I intend to go to my grave as a man of my word. So, consider this a bonus for you helping a friend."

Leaving the astounded attorney with seventy-five grand, Double-O exited the building with a euphoric feeling. While some found joy in alcohol and narcotics, Double-O was addicted to the high that came from being honorable.

Double-O's next stop was at a well-kept cemetery, where he visited the gravesite of his best friend, King.

"What's good, my baby?" he quietly spoke, standing before the headstone with his hands in his pockets. "I apologize for not coming sooner, but I don't be knowing what to say. 'Cause it's like, ain't nothing gon' bring you back, and I ain't even sure if you can hear me."

He drew a deep breath and slowly exhaled. "Bro, I hate to bring you a burden, but we fucked up bad when we went against the grain. 'Cause come to find out, Puma and Kavoni had our best interests at heart. But we got so caught up with wanting to be in charge, that we violated the code we vowed to live by: N-Never F-Forsake Love or L-Loyalty."

It was four years ago, at Wayne County jail, when Double-O had crept into Kavoni's cell with a large knife and a deadly message. "This earth ain't big enough for the both of us." From where he sat on the floor in a state of distress,

Kavoni had looked up at him with tears-stained eyes and encouraged Double-O to make it quick. "They done took my baby brother, butchered my best friend, and now got my lil' mans ready to do me in. I ain't got nothing left to live for, so do what you came to do."

Confused by Kavoni's statements, as Double-O believed he was responsible for the death of his own little brother, he couldn't help but inquire about who Kavoni was referring to. There was a brief lapse of silence before Kavoni answered, "Mecca and Unique."

Double-O was now even more confused. He knew Unique had been King's girl, but didn't understand how Mecca was tied in. As Kavoni took in the expression of a man who didn't have a clue, he blew Double-O's mind when he further revealed, "Mecca and Unique sisters, lil' bruh. They was plotting on us the whole time."

Kavoni then went on to explain the entire ordeal, beginning with the house fire that started it all. As a disbelieving Double-O had dropped the knife and slowly slid down the wall, he gripped his hair in both hands and banged his head into the concrete behind him. Whether it was knowingly or not, the reality was that he had played a major role in his team being defeated. So, unless he could resurrect his friends and set Kavoni free, forgiving himself was unlikely to ever happen.

Repressing bitter memories of a past he couldn't change, Double-O withdrew his hands from his jacket and bent before King's headstone. "I brought you something." He smiled, holding the N.F.L. chain his friend once adored. "Remember how excited we was when Kavoni first gave us these? Nigga, we slept in 'em and swore we would never take 'em off. And it's like the moment we did..." Double-O dropped his head in a gesture of regret. "Is the moment when our ship started to sink."

"It's so crazy, bro," Double-O continued, "'cause I never pictured you going before me. I always thought we would go together, or I'd go protecting you. So just know, I'd trade places with you in a heartbeat if it meant bringing you back. You the closest friend I ever had, my baby, and it really ain't no fun without you here."

In conclusion, Double-O informed King that him and Kavoni were back on righteous terms. "And I'ma do everything I can to get him back on these streets. And that promise I made about making them bitches pay for what they did to our family, I'm standing on that with my whole hundred and sixty-five pounds!"

After glancing over his shoulder, Double-O removed a tool from inside his jacket and dug up a small patch of turf. Dropping the chain in the hole and replacing the dirt, the jewelry piece was now where it rightly belonged.

"A'ight, bro, I'm 'bout to move around," he said, standing back up. "But I love you from the heart, and until I'm called to come join you, rest easy, my baby."

While wearily walking across the recently mowed lawn, Double-O pulled on his hood as it started to rain. Although he wasn't a spiritual person, the sudden downpour implanted the thought that maybe the Heavens could feel his pain.

En route to a separate cemetery to make his peace with Puma, Double-O was vibing to EST GEE as he raced down the rain-slicked road of I-75.

"Is it a place other than hell or jail you get to go when you thorough/ for all the niggas who meant well but failed cause wasn't nobody tryna hear 'em..."

Chapter 13

"Oh my God!" Lo-Lo covered her mouth in shock at the sight of the building Asha had bought and renovated. Finished in a blushing pink, what caressed Lo-Lo's soul was the sizeable sign that sat over the entrance. Lo-Lo turned to eye Asha in pure adoration. "You named it Skittles," she said in reference to the colorful sign.

"You my sister, and I love you," Asha replied. "And what Double-O once say? 'Words are beautiful, but actions are Supreme'." After squeezing each other in a long embrace, Asha took her by the hand. "Come on, let me show you the inside."

Lo-Lo couldn't believe her eyes as they entered the spacious establishment. Bearing an upscale layout, the place was mainly white, with rainbow accents. There were a number of tables considerately spaced; several stages strategically placed; and six elevated VIP booths on either side of the room.

"Girl, you did all this?" Lo-Lo inquired in sheer disbelief.

"With D'Aura's help and a interior designer."

Slowly shaking her head, Lo-Lo continued to marvel at what clearly cost a fortune. And it was named Skittles. "A place like this gon' definitely bring out a certain crowd."

"And that was the goal," Asha said.

Once they'd taken a tour of the entire building, Asha revealed the date on which they would open for business.

"That's perfect!" Lo-Lo approved. "And it'll be a night neither of us will ever forget."

Dizzy with excitement as she pranced to the car, Lo-Lo suddenly grabbed Asha around the waist and picked her up. "Oooh, I can't believe you!" she joyfully exclaimed while swinging Asha around in a circle.

Giggling in delight as Lo-Lo let her down, Asha admitted it had been a tough secret to keep. "There were so many times when I wanted to yell you, but I knew if I waited 'til it was over, your reaction would be priceless. And look... I got you out here swinging me around like I'm a little girl, or something."

With Asha behind the wheel as they rode through downtown, she smiled at Lo-Lo's nonstop rambling. From promotional ideas to DJ recruiting, the girl could've hosted an auction; the way her mouth was moving at a thousand words a minute.

"'Cause see, the thing is..." Lo-Lo paused in mid-sentence as something dawned on her. "Girl, we ain't even got no employees yet. Have you already taken care of that, too?"

"Nope."

"Nope?" Lo-Lo repeated. "Well, what you gon' do?"

"Nah, what *you* gon' do?" Asha corrected her. "You know more about this than I do. So, I'm leaving all the hiring and firing up to you."

Stamping her feet on the floorboard in excitement, Lo-Lo let out a squeal before leaning over to grab Asha's face and kiss her cheek. "You little sneaky girl, you. You should be ashamed of yourself for making me feel this good. Don't you know this people have heart attacks?"

As she envisioned the elite who would soon sit in attendance, Lo-Lo couldn't wait for the grand opening. "I promise you, love, we gon' have the littest shit in the city. I'm talking bad Barbies only. And I already got the perfect place to start."

***

Rocking an Amiri denim ensemble and Red Bottom footwear, Lo-Lo was leaning against a burnt-orange Corvette as two women exited her former place of employment. While both were beautiful, one was the hue of a Hershey's, and the other the color of cinnamon.

"Well, well, well," the darker dancer, Raven, teasingly sang. "Look who finally decided to grace us with her presence."

"Better late than never, right?" Lo-Lo smiled, rising off the car to embrace two women she considered close friends.

Despite her humble demeanor and inner-city origin, Lo-Lo was often an object of scorn on account of her complexion. Some were simply too simple to see past her surface and realize she'd survived struggles much similar to their own. But though they might've discredited the degree of her integrity, there was denying the white girl had swag.

Shortly after being hired at her former place of employment, Lo-Lo's swag and stage presence enabled her to net a nightly four-figures. Angrily observed by two other dancers who couldn't keep up, they cornered Lo-Lo in the dressing room and accused her of stealing their most charitable customers. Surrounded, but not backing down, Lo-Lo had been genuinely relieved when Raven intervened.

"It really take two of you hoes for one white girl?" Raven had casually inquired while opening her locker.

"This deer-ass white girl been stealing our customers," one of the women spoke up. "So shit, she might as well be taking the food right out of my kid's mouths."

"Stealing your customers?" Raven laughed. "Bitch, you got jokes. Ain't nobody coming to see them saggy-ass titties. And if your kids eating really based on your dancing, them lil' mu'fuckas in trouble."

As Lo-Lo forced herself not to laugh, the woman whirled on Raven and warned, "Don't disrespect my kids, hoe. I'll go to war about that shit."

Raven slammed her locker and turned to face her. "Don't threaten me with a good time. Now swing, bitch."

Before a blow could be thrown, Raven's friend and fellow dancer, Kiva, hurried into the dressing room to change her outfit. But when she noticed the two women standing toe-to-toe, she changed directions and quickly put her hair into a ponytail. "Wassup, Ray-Ray, what this hoe on?"

A deadly mixture of Puerto Rican and black, Kiva was just as gangster as she was gorgeous. And it was widely known she kept a razor in her cheek and pepper spray in her purse. Which was the woman wisely decided this was a war not worth waging.

"Kiva, you know me and you ain't never had a problem," she cowardly said in a respectful tone.

"We will if you got one with my girl. So move around before your shit need stitches. And don't let it happen again. Cause this your first and *only* warning."

As the two weasels practically ran out the room, Lo-Lo joined Ray-Ray and Kiva in laughter. And that memorable night marked the beginning of a friendship between her and two strangers who saw past her skin and into the pureness of her heart. And it was for that reason she presently stood before them with a business proposal that would upgrade their lives.

"Y'all ready to make some real money?" Lo-Lo asked, looking at both women. "Or y'all trying to be dancing up in there till you thirty?"

Kiva nudged her head at the burnt orange coup. "What's that a rental?"

Lo-Lo reached in her pocket and pulled out the pink slip. "Since when did Enterprise start passing these out?"

Instructing the women to trail her in their car, Lo-Lo led them to a nearby White Castle, where they continued the conversation at a table in the back.

"So, it's this plush ass spot that's finna open downtown," Lo-Lo explained. "I'm talking about something you'd see on TV. It's gon' separate the ballers from the bums. And I want y'all to come dance there. It'll have less girls, which means more money."

Ray-Ray was on the verge of speaking, when Lo-Lo cut her off with additional information. "Oh, and I forgot to mention, on Saturday nights... you keep what you make."

Both women eyed her in disbelief, with Ray-Ray replying, "Girl, everybody and they mama know Saturday night do numbers. And you sitting here telling me we get to keep how much we make?"

Lo-Lo raised her right hand and solemnly swore, "Y'all ain't never known me to do no capping. If it's five thousand you make, it's five thousand you take."

"Yeah, but what's the catch?" Kiva questioned in skepticism, "cause if this joint gon' jump like you say, then there's gotta be a trick to it. Something you might not know about. Lo-Lo, you know I love you, girl, but I ain't playing about my money."

Leaning forward, Lo-Lo grasped their hand and came from the heart. "I understand y'all cautious, 'cause I would be too. But the fact is, y'all was there for me when it mattered, and you didn't even know me. I literally grew up in the same slums and endured the same struggles, but you know how many women be dogging me out? Just because I'm white."

Lo-Lo teared-up but continued, "but y'all didn't judge me by that. You saw me for who I am, which is another woman who just trying to make it. And you'll never know how much I appreciate you for that. 'Cause to step in for a stranger is unheard of in this day and age. So I also gotta acknowledge y'all for who y'all are, which are pure-hearted women who deserve to win. And now that I'm in a better position, that's what I intend to do... see you win. And my word as a woman, ain't no catch."

Moved by her heartfelt disclosure, both women lovingly squeezed Lo-Lo's hand. They felt her. And they were both currently thinking along the lines. That the girl was indeed dipped in designer, and had produced the pink slip to a six-figure coup. But more importantly, she had never gave one indication she was unworthy of being trusted. In their upper twenties with under ten in their savings, what was there to lose?

"So, when you say this spot finna open?" Ray-Ray smiled at Lo-Lo, leaning over the table to hug her.

"Less than two weeks!" Lo-Lo beamed.

Kiva was looking at Lo-Lo as if she was still unsure, then couldn't hold it in no longer and bursted out in laughter. "Girl, you know you better count me in," she raised her hand for a high-five. " 'Cause I see me in a Tesla this summer!"

They were leaving the restaurant, when Lo-Lo informed them of a mandatory meeting the following Monday. "Besides going over some paperwork, it's somebody I want y'all to meet."

Exchanging hugs before heading to their cars, Lo-Lo awakened her supercharged engine with a touch of a button. Upon sliding inside and fastening her seatbelt, she double tapped the horn and left streaks in the street as the 'Vette fishtailed out the parking lot. Reaching 0-60 in under four seconds, she was flying down Seven Mile, when she got an incoming call from an unknown number.

She touched the screen on the dash and curiously answered, "Hello?"

"What up doe?" Uno's voice came through the car speakers.

"Boy, what I tell you?" Lo-Lo laughed. "Now I'ma have to block you and go downtown."

"I'm saying, you was taking too long, you feel me. So I got kinda worried about you and just wanted to check up on you. That's all. Can't fault a man for being concerned."

"Uno, it's only been a few days since we saw each other."

"Yeah, but we in the "D" , my baby, and you know how this shit go. Mu'fucka be here today and be getting buried tomorrow. But I'm saying though, where you at right now?"

"On my way home."

"I'm trying to see you. Let's link up right quick."

"It's almost three in the morning. Maybe tomorrow or something."

"This ain't no booty-call, yo. This just me trying to get to know you. And I'm saying, you up, I'm up, so why not link up?

As Lo-Lo contemplated in confliction, Uno humorously added, "We can meet across the street from the precinct, if that'll make you feel more comfortable. I'm just trying to sit in the car and chill, and find out your real name, favorite color, goals in life, and whatever else you willing to tell a nigga. Let me show you I'm different, my baby."

Knowing Asha would disapprove of her decision, Lo-Lo found herself asking him where he wanted to meet. And as she deviated from the direction of her house, she had no idea of the damaging affect her decision would have on the Butterfly Mafia.

Chapter 14

Inside a backroom at Skittles, a dozen women were seated on either side of a conference table. With Noni seated at her right and Lo-Lo to the left, Asha sat at the head of the polished slab.

"I wanna thank everyone for coming out on such short notice," Asha addressed the dancers Lo-Lo had handpicked. Despite their complexions ranging from pink to purple, all twelve were gorgeous as hell. "As you know, this club finna open in less than two weeks now. And our goal gotta be to generate as much money as possible. I want us to eventually have people coming from all over the Midwest. And the only way to do that is by working together as a team. So if you gotta idea, share it. If you ain't feeling something, speak up. 'Cause the thing is, the more money thrown is the more you take home. And I'm sure Lo-Lo told you Saturday nights is all yours."

Amid nods of approval and appreciative smiles, Ray-Ray raised her hand. "Yo, I gotta keep it a buck, my baby. Lo-Lo my girl, but I was lightweight leery when she told me about that. 'Cause I've been doing this for a minute, and I ain't never heard no shit like that."

Kiva won Asha's favor when she chimed in, "What she really wanna to say is, we trying to hear it straight from the horse's mouth. So, is you the owner if this joint or what?"

"I am," Asha answered. "Along with my two sisters right here. So whatever Lo-Lo told you is what you can take to the bank."

Ray-Ray and Kiva looked at Lo-Lo in surprise, with Kiva teasing, "Dag, girl, you could've told us you was gon' be our boss."

"Aye, I ain't trying to be all up in y'all business," a caramel-complected woman spoke up, "but it ain't no mystery y'all names ringing out here in these streets. So I'm just wondering if everything on the up-and-up with this spot. Far as liquor license, safety permits, and whatnot. 'Cause I'm knocking nobody, but I can't afford to be getting caught up in no conspiracies. My baby daddy doing twenty in the feds for that right now."

Kiva leaned forward to look down the table. "Damn, bitch, is you the police? Asking all them retarded ass questions."

"Nah, I'ma mother," she clarified with emphasis. "And I can't do shit for my child if I'm locked the fuck up. So I appreciate the invite, but I'd rather stay where I am before I get jammed up in some other shit."

Asha raised a hand for silence. "She gotta point. Because the same way she can't care for her seed if she in a cage, is the same way I can't make money if I'm her codefendant."

There was a knock at the door and Asha gestured for Noni to go open it. It was D'Aura, who rolled in a cart that had an ice cooler on top.

"I don't judge nobody besides rats and pedophiles," Asha said, as the women eyed the cooler in curiosity. "But there's certain things I can't allow in this club. And that's sex and drugs. They'll shut this shit down in a heartbeat. So if you wanna make extra money on the side, I don't encourage it, but I understand sometimes you gotta what you feel is necessary. It just can't happen up in Skittles. And far as drugs, that's a definite no-no."

With that said, D'Aura opened the cooler and began removing clear, lidded cups, which she placed on the conference table.

"Is this what I think it is?" the concerned mother rhetorically asked, picking up one of the cups.

"It's a piss test," Noni spat. Her patience with the woman was already wearing thin. "So if you piss dirty for anything other than weed, we can't do shit for you but point you to rehab.

"But if a person ain't bringing nothing into the club, then what that gotta do with them dancing?" the mother protested.

"Aw, ain't this some shit," Kiva sat back and chuckled. "This hoe did all that hollering about taking care of her kid, and she a fucking junkie. Wow!"

"Bitch, I ain't no fucking junkie."

"Then prove it and piss in the cup then."

"Listen, like my sister said, we ain't here to look down on nobody or judge them," Lo-Lo cut in. "But what I know from personal experience is that when a person hooked on hard drugs, when they need it they need it, and it don't matter where they at. My mama OD'd from that shit, so I know what I'm talking about. 'Cause she would've pulled out her kit in church to scratch that itch. Now y'all gotta understand, me and my sisters built this shit from the ground up. By our hands alone. So ain't no way we finna let nobody tear it down over something we can avoid."

"So if it's anybody here who need time to clean up, just come back when you ready," Asha reasoned. "We'll put you on a 30-day probationary period, and if you drop clean again, you hired. Simple as that."

"So what, y'all gon' stand there and watch us piss in the cup?" the mother asked, as if she was offended by the idea.

Fed up, Noni scooted her chair back and stood. "What, you think we ain't never been locked up? You think we don't know you'll give us some baby piss? I guess you think we made it this far by being dumb as fuck, huh?"

Asha laid a calming hand in her sister's arm. "It's okay, love."

"Yeah, I'm most definitely cool on all this," the woman rose from the table and began gathering her things. "Lo-Lo, I appreciate the offer, but y'all on some other shit up in here."

"Nah, *you* on some other shit!" Noni barked. " 'Cause ain't no other club on planet earth finna let you keep all your money on no Saturday night. And all we asking for in return is some fucking piss. But you ain't even woman enough to be like, 'Damn, this worth me getting my shit together. This my chance to see some serious paper. So let me stop getting high for a minute.'

Noni gave her a vicious once-over, then snorted in contempt, "Yeah, you definitely cut from a different cloth. So get your weak ass up outta here."

Asha caught up with the woman as she angrily left the room. "Listen, I know my twin's approach is kinda harsh, but if you got any realness in you, then you'll accept the truth in what she said about this being an opportunity worth getting clean for. Cause whether it be for good or bad, life involves sacrifices, love. So you gotta decide what you wanna do, while you still got time to do it."

Asha then wrote down her number and encouraged the woman to use it. "You a beautiful girl, and I already know you'll have 'em digging deep in they pockets. So I'm hoping you'll end up doing the right thing. And if you need help in the process, call my number day or night, and we'll figure it out."

The woman saw the sincerity in Asha's eyes. "You really mean that, don't you?"

"Wholeheartedly. I wish I could save every struggling girl in the world. But since I can't, I can only help the ones I run across. So like I said, don't hesitate to call me."

The two women hugged before Asha watched her walk to her car and drive off. She could only hope that in the end the woman's ambition would overpower her addiction.

Reentering the room, Asha asked if there was anyone else who needed time to rearrange their priorities.

A red-haired white girl stuck her hand up. "I powder my nose on occasion, so I might drop dirty for cocaine."

Asha looked to Lo-Lo, who factually stated, "She'll be cool in a few days, long as she don't do no more."

"You heard her," Asha returned her attention to Red. "So if you serious, come back in a few. But I'm warning you now, I'ma be dropping you randomly. And if you drop dirty, you'll be suspended for a month."

Red bobbed her head in understanding. "Alright, I got you. I'ma tighten up. Cause I've been wanting to leave that shit alone anyway. And what better motive than money."

"I need y'all to understand something," Asha swept her gaze over the table, "everything we got came straight out the mud. Ain't no father, uncle, or boyfriend helped us get nothing. So we just trying to protect our first and only investment. So don't take this personal, but try and see our perspective. And let's make more money than we ever had."

As the remaining women were individually entering the restroom with Lo-Lo and providing urine samples, Noni and Kiva were chatting it up like old friends. Both were equally outspoken, and Kiva had a family member who was a stud. So, she already knew what to expect. But she had to admit that Noni was in a league of her own. For there weren't many women who had the stare of a wild animal. While Kiva considered herself a warrior, she regarded her new friend for what she was, a cold-hearted murderer.

Wearing a blank expression as she quietly observed the room, Asha was actually bubbling with excitement on the inside. In just two more days it would be May 25th... the day on which Shawna was scheduled to be released from rehab.

Chapter 15

As they stood at the rear of the Denali, Asha, Lo-Lo, and Noni's heartbeats were hammering with anticipation. At any second, their fourth wing would officially join them on their journey through life.

When Shawna exited the rehab facility minutes later, carrying her belongings in a suitcase, she showcased every tooth she had at the sight of her sisters. While this was a moment she had envisioned for months, there wasn't a word in a Webster to define her inner joy.

Lacking the discipline to detain her excitement, Shawna literally dropped her suitcase and bolted into their outstretched arms.

Angel was planted outside the front entrance, from where she used her phone to record their tearful reunion. And while it warmed her heart, she felt a tinge of jealousy over their sisterly bond; as it was something she longed to be a part of.

As the four girls spoke words of endearment and wiped at each other's eyes, Shawna bursted out in laughter, prompting the others to join in. "Oh my God!" Shawna fanned her face, attempting to regulate her breathing. "I'ma mess around and have an asthma attack, and I ain't even got asthma."

After another light chuckle, Shawna seriously stated, "but for real, y'all, I can't even tell you how happy I am to be standing here right now. This literally a dream come true.

Y'all all I got, but all I need. And I give you my word on all four wings, I won't let you down."

Shawna's declaration called for another group hug.

"Come on, we gotta go, y'all." Lo-Lo looked at her watch. They had Shawna's first day out planned to a *T*.

With Asha claiming the wheel and Shawna her designated passenger, the four women piled inside the SUV. It rolled forward several feet before the brake lights flashed and it quickly reversed. Noni hopped out to retrieve Shawna's nearly forgotten suitcase, oblivious of Angel as she stared in their direction.

When Noni hopped back in the truck and it sped off, a tear of hurt and anger slid down Angel's face. She desperately wanted to be a member of the Butterfly Mafia, as her own friends failed to measure up to their level of loyalty and substance. After her role in the unarmed robberies of the men in California and Miami, Angel was certain that would've earned her a seat on their council. But as she turned to head back inside the facility, she was beginning to wonder if she'd been used to their advantage.

"When We Ride" by Tokyo Jetz was bumping inside the truck as Asha punched it down I-75. As she steered with her left hand and slightly leaned to the right, Shawna's head was subtle bobbing to the beat while she gazed out at the passing scenery. And in the backseat, Noni kept glancing at Lo-Lo, who was busily texting on her phone. Lo-Lo would occasionally grin, to which Noni correctly assumed was a reaction to a response from Uno.

A few hours later, they arrived in Columbus, Ohio, the state's capital. GPS guided them to an indoor/outdoor mall called Easton, where Asha backed into a space on the lower level of the parking garage.

Before exiting the truck, Noni slipped the strap of a designer bag over her shoulder. Every bill in the satchel would be spent on Shawna's wardrobe.

As they marched through the mall, with their magnetic presence drawing a number of stares, Asha quietly encouraged Shawna to get whatever she wanted. "It's like $25,000 in Noni's bag, and we expect you to spend every dime of it."

Visiting various high-end boutiques, Shawna's purchases required them to make multiple trips back-and-forth to the truck. "I don't think we can fit nothing else in here," Shawna said, as she stared at the trunk full of bags. "And I already got every outfit and shoe I can possibly think of."

Noni withdrew the last stack from the bag and rifled through it. "Well, it's like a couple thousand left, so you better think of something."

Shawna looked at Asha, who shrugged in response, "I told you, love, you gotta -"

Asha's voice trailed off at the piercing scream of small child.

"Little girl, if you don't stop, I'ma snatch a knot in your ass and give you something to really cry about," a woman threatened, as she drug the child along by her wrist.

"Ma'am," Shawna intervened, unable to stomach another second of the sickening scene.

"Yes?" she whirled on Shawna with a wild-eyed expression. "Can I help you with something?"

Noni went to step forward but Asha grabbed her; for she was curious to see how Shawna handled the situation.

"She look just like you, so I'm assuming that's your child," Shawna replied in a mild mannered tone.

The woman frowned in uncertainty, as she took in Shawna and the three other girls. "Yeah, this my child."

"She so pretty," Shawna smiled in adoration of the pint-sized girl. "Can I have her? I'll pay you whatever price you name."

"Hell nah, you can't buy my child!" the woman protectively placed her daughter behind her. "What type of mother you think I am?"

"Ma'am, I didn't mean no harm," Shawna quickly put her hands up in apology. "But you were being so mean to her. I just thought that maybe you didn't want her no more. 'Cause my mama used to treat me the same way, and she always reminded me of how much she hated me and wish she could rid of me. So I only thought I'd be doing you a favor, that's all. And I'm sorry if I offended you."

At the reflection of purity in Shawna's dove-like eyes, the woman lowered her gaze and wearily sighed. She was wrong and she knew it.

"I just get so frustrated sometimes," she found herself confessing to a total stranger. "I'm doing everything on my own, and her daddy won't help. So whenever she ask for something, which I can never afford, it just make me hate him even more for leaving me to struggle like this. And I guess it's like, since I can't take it out on him, I take it out on the closest thing to him." The woman looked down to regard her daughter with a look of remorse. "And that ain't right, because she ain't even ask to be here."

Shawna sensed that the woman didn't harbor a hateful heart. But like so many others, she was simply striving to swim through what seemed to be a never ending struggle. And though it was a tiresome battle, you had to search inward and find a reason to live; so as not to become fully submerged in the sea of bitterness.

"What was it she wanted?" Shawna inquired.

"Girl, some Barbie doll she saw in the store."

Shawna turned to Noni, who wordlessly reached in the bag.

Turning back to the woman, Shawna held out the loaf of bread. "Here, I want you to have this. It'll take care of the doll, and a few other things you might need."

The woman looked at both Shawna and the money in disbelief. "Are you sure?"

"Absolutely. But I want you always remember something. One day she gon' grow up to be a woman, and it's your job to make she get there as ladylike as possible."

After watching the woman and child reenter the mall, Asha praised Shawna with a proud smile, "That was beautiful, love. And me being honest, I don't think either one of us could've did a better job."

"For real," Lo-Lo agreed. "Because any other approach probably wouldn't have gotten through to her. So yeah, that was definitely well-delivered."

As they rode in silence to their next destination, Shawna was reflecting on a segment of her past, when Puma's compassion had rescued her. So though her road to redemption was considerably long, gratitude gave her the spirit to assist who she could along the way.

Arriving at an inner city beauty salon, they were just in time for Shawna's afternoon appointment. Asha had googled several salons weeks in advance, with this being the building that earned the most favorable reviews.

When they entered the crowded shop, all chatter receded into a curious silence. Aside from the girls looking good in their fashionable fabrics, they stepped with a seasoned swagger and unspoken unity.

At the front counter, Asha informed an employee of Shawna's appointment.

"And what's the last name?"

"Perry. Shawna Perry."

She marked off the name with a yellow highlighter, and pointed out a brown skin woman across the room. "Go to her right there."

Introducing herself as Clarissa, she asked Shawna what she wanted as she sat in the chair. "

"Uhm..." she stammered, not knowing how to respond.

"Give her a sidepiece sew-in," Lo-Lo spoke up. "And like 30-inches of that good Brazilian shit. We gotta get her ready for a photoshoot."

Shawna shot Lo-Lo an appreciative smile, to which Lo-Lo winked in response. It had slipped their minds that this was likely Shawna's first time attending a salon.

Ever alert, Noni noticed a woman who kept cutting her eyes at Lo-Lo with a look of distaste. It made her sick to her stomach when they hated on her girl just because she was white.

"Excuse me," Noni waved for the woman's attention. When they locked eyes, Noni blatantly asked her, "why you keep checking out my sister? I'm saying, is you trying to fight her or fuck her?"

The shop instantly went mute at the bold and unexpected inquiry. Even Asha had been caught off guard.

The hater screwed up her face and sassily replied, "For one, I ain't gay. And two, if I was, I damn sure wouldn't be with no Karen, Becky, or whatever the fuck her white ass name is. Up in this bitch talking 'bout a sidepiece sew-in. What y'all do, rehearse that shit before you got here?"

There were scattered chuckles throughout the shop.

Although Lo-Lo was accustomed to the scornful comments, they still somehow managed to hurt her feelings each time. Because in spite of her ties to the trenches, she had never intentionally attempted to mimic a black girl's behavior. If only people would acknowledge that any non-black person who grew up in the slums would adopt certain ways of a contagious culture.

Masking her anger with an unamused chuckle, Noni scanned the room. While what she was doing may have went unnoticed by everyone else, Asha knew exactly what was on her twin's mind.

Upon completion of her sew-in, Shawna looked in the mirror and couldn't believe her eyes. She looked so...different. With a glow on her skin from the time spent in rehab, the hairstyle highlighted her chocolate pie face.

Shawna was paying the stylist, when Noni drew several stares as she abruptly left the shop.

Outside at the truck, Noni reached under her seat and felt around until her hand came into contact with the micro Hellcat. There were no cameras in the shop, and she intended to teach the hater two valuable lessons: never take life for granted, and sometimes our actions are rewarded with swift repercussions.

Wedging the weapon in her waistband, Noni turned to go back inside and literally ran into Asha. "Really, Noni? You really about to go back in there and do that in front of all them people?"

"We ain't even from here," Noni stubbornly replied. "And it ain't even no cameras in there."

"Girl, what you think them people is? They cameras that can talk! I know you upset, but don't let emotion make you do something we all gon' end up regretting."

"She right, love." Lo-Lo walked up. "And it ain't even worth it. 'Cause if we did something to everybody that had something slick to say about me, we'd be serial killers. So fuck 'em. We got love and respect for each other, and that's really all that matters."

As Noni eyed the sidewalk in deep thought, Shawna softly pitched in, "I love you, Noni."

Lo-Lo hit Shawna with her elbow, to which she shrugged her shoulders; for that was all she could think of to say at the moment.

Bearing a slight frown as she looked up at Shawna, Noni said, "I love you, too," then sidestepped Asha and reentered the salon.

With all eyes on her, Noni blew down on the hater and told her to stand up. When she bravely complied, Noni drew her weapon with swiftness of a cowboy.

As people gasped in shock, Noni was thrilled by the split second change in the hater's demeanor. The confident look had been replaced with undressed fear; which meant she'd make for a superb listener.

"Look at me," Noni instructed, aligning her firearm with the woman's forehead. When she timidly obeyed, Noni continued, "You got kids?"

She nodded.

"How many?"

"Three," she answered barely above a whisper.

Noni scoffed, "I got double that in bodies. And if it wasn't for that white girl you hate for no reason, I'd add you to my count and turn your kids into orphans."

With her weapon extended as she reversed to the door, Noni let herself out and jogged to truck. Asha skirted off before her door fully shut.

After showing up late to Shawna's nail appointment, where she got a full set with butterfly designs, they went to a tattoo parlor on the west side.

Choosing a female artist who was beautifully sprayed, Asha introduced her to Shawna and explained what they had in mind. The artist thoughtfully nodded before asking Shawna where she wanted the piece.

"Anywhere where it won't hurt that bad."

The tattooist laughed out loud. "I'm sorry, sweetie, but it's gon' hurt pretty much anywhere you get it. But I would advise you to avoid the stomach and back area."

Shawna settled on the inside of her right forearm.

With her eyes shut tight as she sat in the chair, Shawna was wincing and groaning while gripping Asha's hand. Though it wasn't that long, it felt as if she'd been in the chair for hours.

"I'm almost done, sweetie," the lady consoled, freehanding a piece that was turning out impressive.

When she finally rolled back in her chair and announced she was finished, all three girls closed in on Shawna and studied the drawing of a floating butterfly. Above it were the initials "B.F.M.", and beneath it was Shawna's permanent pledge, "For Life".

Squealing in delight, they engaged in a group hug; for Shawna was now an official member of The Butterfly Mafia.

While headed back to their hometown, they showered Shawna in praise and adoration. And as she bathed in the bliss of their genuine love, she could've never predicted that her loyalty would encounter an unthinkable test.

Chapter 16

"So, why haven't you convinced your sister to let me join y'all yet?" Angel asked Noni, as they stood outside her job at the rehab facility. On her lunch break, Angel had a lit cigarette pinched between her fingers. Smoking was something she did only when seriously upset.

"Man, that's what you called me all the way up here for?" Noni replied. "About some shit that could've waited till you got off work?"

"I'm tired of fucking waiting! I've done everything there is to prove I'm worthy of being a member. And I don't it's fair that—"

"You don't think it's fair that what?" Noni implored as Angel stopped in mid-sentence. "Gone and say it. You don't think it's fair that what?"

She sucked on the cigarette before shaking her head. "Nah, don't even worry about it. 'Cause I shouldn't have to beg to be a part of something I helped build."

"You helped build?" Noni lifted her eyebrows. "Are you fucking serious?"

"Abso-fucking-lutely. Because one," Angel stuck out her thumb, "I introduced y'all to my brother. And everybody know connections like that are hard to come across. Especially for a group of girls. And two," she extended her forefinger, "that shit that happened out in Cali and Miami couldn't have happened without this Mexican girl. And if my family knew I used pictures of my dead father, they'd disown me for sure. So yeah, I think that entitles me to a seat at the table."

Noni just nodded in response, inwardly thinking of how spoiled this girl was. Everything in life had been freely given to her, which blinded her to the reality that with certain people certain things had to be earned, such as trust. If Asha had foresaw Angel's feelings of entitlement, she hadn't mentioned it. So Noni would keep it kosher until they could talk. She just hoped her sister had a precooked remedy, for she could sense this was a situation that would soon boil over.

"Yeah, you right," Noni conceded, lightly touching Angel's arm. " 'Cause you have come through on everything we asked you to. So I'ma definitely sit my sister down and make her listen."

"You mean that?"

Noni nodded, "I do."

Angel regarded her for a moment before suggesting, "Then, prove it."

"How?"

She flicked the cancer stick and stepped closer to Noni. "Come over tonight and make me scream. Make me remember why I'm so patient with you."

Wrinkling her nose at Angel's nicotine scented breath, Noni answered, "That might not be a good idea right now."

"And why not?" Angel frowned, wondering if Noni had found someone else.

Forgetful of Asha's counsel, Noni made a crucial mistake by telling the truth. "Let's just say your brother ain't too fond of us mixing business with pleasure."

"I don't believe you." Angel defensively crossed her arms.

"Alright." Noni shrugged, recalling the conversation between her and Perez. "But I ain't got no reason to lie. And if you really serious about this Mob shit, then you should understand my position. 'Cause the growth of our sisterhood outweighs everything."

Leaving Angel with a kiss on the cheek and a promise to call her later, Noni hopped back in the rental and pulled off.

Angel made a brief phone call before returning to work. "We need to talk," she said to the person on the other end.

***

Later that evening, Angel came out her condo and climbed in the backseat of a Cadillac Escalade.

"So, what's so urgent that I had to put business on hold?" Perez inquired as she settled beside him.

"Why would you discourage Noni from wanting to be with me? When you slept with some of my friends in the past, I didn't say anything. But now that I've found someone that I really like, you gotta problem with it."

"Angel, I have no idea on what you're talking about," he lied without batting an eye. "You're a grown woman, whose love life has nothing to do with me. As long as your wellbeing isn't in jeopardy, then you can date whoever you want."

"Yeah, well, she said you didn't want her mixing business with pleasure."

"And I say she trying to use me as a way to avoid you. Because think about it, my business arrangement is with her sister."

Angel stared at her lap in deep contemplation. If her brother was being truthful, which he normally was, then that just confirmed her suspicions of Noni seeing someone else. And maybe she was also right in regards to being used to their advantage. But what she couldn't understand was why Noni would use her brother as an excuse, when he was someone she could so easily question.

"You're overthinking something so simple," Perez reached over to take her hand. "See this as a sign instead of a setback. Because I did my research on that girl, Noni. And I'm told she's as heartless as any hitman I've ever hired. So while I can tell you got feelings for her, it would be naive of you to think that someone like her would be capable of reciprocating those same feelings. It's just not who she is, sis'."

Angel quickly wiped away a fallen tear. "But I can't understand why she'd lie to me. She could've just told me she only wanted to be friends, and I would've accepted that."

Observing her sadness in genuine remorse, Perez was only doing what their father would want, protecting his sister from probable harm. With Dullah's death being the most recent addition, Asha and Noni were rumored to have murdered a number of men. But as Perez knew, gangsters were rarely awarded long runs. So he would ensure that his sister was safe when their race inevitably came to an end; even it meant giving gas to the process.

Chapter 17

Like a streak of lightning, Lo-Lo's supercharged Stingray zipped down a darkened highway at nearly triple digits. Behind the wheel was Asha, who was en route to a secret residence in a neighboring city.

As she got off on an exit in Pontiac, Michigan, Asha checked the rearview for a sign of trailing headlights. Without a pair in sight, she drove to a suburban section of the small city, where she pulled into the driveway of a light-blue house and parked around back.

Unlocking the glovebox, she withdrew a 10-round Ruger, disengaged its safety and departed the coup. This was an instance that required abnormal alertness and split second reflexes.

Once safely inside the fully furnished house, which Asha had leased for the next six months, she deactivated the alarm and stood deathly still. When her instincts announced she was alone in the house, she stuffed the semi in her pants and went upstairs.

Approaching the door to the master bedroom, she grasped the knob, inhaled a calming breath, then slowly opened it and peeked inside. As usual, she experienced a euphoric feeling upon viewing the room. Free of furniture, the expansive enclosure resembled a drug lord's dumping ground; as the carpet was covered in colorful currency.

With the success of their trap house raking in trash bags of cash, Asha knew the significance of stashing their savings at a safe and secure site. So until she could cleanse the money of its illegal grime, she settled on a suburban location in a nearby city.

Literally walking on money, she went to the closet and grabbed two large duffel bags. After stuffing them both with an unknown amount, she chuckled at the fact that her withdrawal had done very little damage. *All this money*, she smiled in amazement.

With a bag over her shoulder and the other in hand, Asha returned downstairs to the kitchen. She fished her phone from her pocket and pulled up the app to access the camera system. From what the screen reflected - as it provided images of the outside parameter, there were no visible signs that an ambush awaited. Resetting the alarm, she withdrew her weapon and exited the house.

Watchful as ever as she walked to the car, Asha was tossing the second bad inside, when her heartbeat froze from a noise behind her. With a ballerina's grace, she crouched and spun in one swift motion.

His marble-like eyes shining bright in the night, the adversary before her was a motionless skunk. Well aware of what he'd do if frightened, Asha calmly encouraged the bushy-tailed fellow to keep his cool. "I don't want no smoke with you, lil' buddy." She slowly raised her hands in a surrendering gesture. "So I'ma just be on my way."

Their stares never strayed as she eased into the car.

Once she was tucked inside with the door closed and locked, Asha laid a hand of relief over her thumping heart. She laughed in amusement as she brought the coup to a start. Of all the dangerous scenarios her mind had considered, she had never thought to include an encounter with the foul-smelling mammal.

As Asha raced back to Detroit with a car full of cash, she was thinking about the means in which she'd clean the money. Though it was simple, it was guaranteed to work. And as she grew excited by its visualization, she bore further down on the gas and made the Stingray scream like a scalded dog.

Chapter 18

"You sure you don't need me to come with you?" Asha asked Shawna as they sat parked in front of her grandmother's house.

Eyeing the house in dread, Shawna slowly shook her head. "As much as I want you to, this a fear I gotta face alone."

Since Shawna's memory had begun to record, she couldn't recall one single episode in which her grandmother had showed her an act of kindness or encouragement. The woman had been relentless with the ridicule, regularly reminding Shawna of her so many imperfections. And when the teasing would take its toll and she'd break down in tears, the woman would curse her for being weak and beat her with whatever within arm's reach.

"Float like a butterfly..." Asha sang to Shawna as she opened the car door. Shawna looked over her shoulder and smiled, "And sting like a bee."

A moment after ringing the doorbell of her grandmother's house, the door cracked open and Shawna came face-to-face with the woman whose presence alone once made her shiver in fear. But no more, Shawna told herself, refusing to cower beneath her grandmother's glare.

"Well, look what decide to show up on my doorstep," the gray-haired woman spat, giving her granddaughter a distasteful once over. "And I ain't never known you to wear nothing nice, so that shit you got on either stolen or borrowed."

The woman looked past Shawna and took in the Denali XL. "I know you ain't had no damn pimp to bring you to my house."

"That's my best friend, and she ain't no pimp," Shawna clarified. "But Granny if I could just grab some of my stuff, I'll be on way."

"What stuff?" she placed a defiant hand on her hips.

"It's just a few things I put up, that all."

Making no move to let her granddaughter in, she happily informed, "I cleared out that room a while back. After I hadn't seen you in so long, I figured you joined your mama, and I donated all that 'stuff' to the goodwill. But I took it to the one right around the corner, if you wanna go check to see if they still got any of it."

Shawna smirked, grateful for being intuitive in the past. "It wasn't in my room, Granny. I put it up downstairs in the basement. So if you'll just let me grab it real quick, I won't take long."

The woman grunted, thoroughly upset by being outwitted. "Well, you can just tell me where it is and I'll go get it. 'Cause I don't need you down there going through all my things. I gotta lotta valuables down there."

Shawna almost laughed in her face, for the only thing of value in the basement was an outdated washer and dryer. "Granny, you can watch me if you want. But I put it up on a shelf. And I wouldn't want you to fall and hurt yourself."

As Shawna could sense the wheels of the woman's mind racing towards rejection, she went in her pocket and pulled out some bills. "For your troubles," she said, enticingly holding in her hand the blue-colored paper.

Her favorite color, the woman feigned annoyance as she unlocked the screen door. "Shawna, I'm telling you now," she plucked the paper from her hand, "I don't want you down there going through all my stuff. So I'm giving you five minutes to get whatever you trying to get."

With her grandmother breathing on her neck, Shawna stacked two crates in front of a shelf in the basement. As her heartbeat hammered in fear and anticipation, fear that it was gone and anticipation that it wasn't, she stepped up on the crates and broadly smiled when seeing the box. *Oh thank you God!* she silently prayed.

"What's in the box?" the woman couldn't help but ask, from the Shawna clutched it to her chest like a precious newborn.

"Just a few personals," she shrugged, returning the crates to their original placement.

"Next time call before you just decide to pop up," the woman fussed at Shawna while trailing her back upstairs. "I could've had company, been sleep, or doing Lord knows what."

Overwhelmed with joy and a lightness of heart, Shawna paused at the door and looked back at her grandmother. "Regardless of how you treated me, I'll always have love for you. 'Cause I'm so glad to be alive now, and my birth couldn't have happened if it wasn't for you. Be well, granny."

Unable to think of a sharp reply, the woman stared after Shawna as she strode to the truck without once looking back. And as much as it pained her to think it, the girl bore an energy that reeked of serenity.

"So how'd it go?" Asha couldn't wait to inquire as she pulled away from the curb.

Staring straight ahead in a thoughtful manner, Shawna answered, "Exactly how I imagined. She ain't changed one bit."

How could a grandmother harbor such hatred for her own grandchild? That was a question Shawna had often asked herself while tearfully curled beneath her covers at night. But now that she was legally of age, and in the greatest mental shape of her life, she decided the woman was a toxin she'd no longer inhale. So unless their paths were to coincidentally cross in public, she had no intentions of revisiting her grandmother's residence ever again.

In the seclusion of her room at the twin's house, Shawna sat on the floor and regarded the box. Even when her addiction had spiraled out of control, she had settled on selling her body, rather than these priceless possessions that memorialized Puma.

Removing a jewelry case from the box, Shawna opened it to reveal a gold necklace with a small diamond pendant in the shape of an *S*. She vividly recalled the summer afternoon when Puma had surprised her with it, and the surreal sensation that came from receiving her very first gift.

After clasping the necklace around her neck, Shawna eyed the Crown Royal bag in the box before carefully removing it. She laid it on the floor, untied its string, and brought into view a full-size Glock. In spite of its menacing appearance, it was actually the closest link to her late friend, Puma. For this had been her beloved pistol she nicknamed Martha.

Gripping the gun in her hand, Shawna closed her eyes and envisioned different images of her and Puma together. From the night they first met, to the day Puma gave her a memorable message: 'Being the underdog just means you gotta walk a little farther and fight a little harder'.

You know I'm not a killer, Shawna inwardly prayed, *but, Lord, if I ever get the chance, I gotta get revenge for what they did to my friend.*

Little did Shawna know, her date with the devil was already set.

Chapter 19

"Where y'all taking me?" Shawna giggled, as she rode blindfolded in the front seat of the hot-pink GTO. Accompanied by her four-girl crew, they were each rocking a white, leather varsity jacket.

As Asha drove through downtown, she looked over to make sure Shawna's blindfold was still intact. "Don't be over there trying to peek."

From in the backseat, Lo-Lo and Noni assured her they'd be there in just a few short minutes. "And this 'bout to blow your whole kufi off!" Noni jokingly added.

The car soon slowed, and Shawna felt the bump of them turning into a parking lot. With her eyes honestly closed, she had no idea of where they were, but could only imagine what they had in store. It was just no telling with these three.

As the car came to a stop, Shawna was told to remove the blindfold. With her heartbeat galloping like a wild horse, she untied the scarf and expressed utter shock.

"Oh. My. God!" she stared in disbelief at Club Skittles. But what really made an impression was the amount of activity currently underway. Along with a parking lot full of foreign sedans and customized old schools, the entrance line was unbelievably long. With armed security in charge of admissions, this was the outside image of a successful business.

Shawna looked at Asha. "Is this really—"

Asha bobbed her head with a 1000-watt smile, "It's really ours, love."

"And this the grand opening," Lo-Lo chipped in. "You know we couldn't do it without you. Welcome home, girl."

Not knowing what to say, Shawna resorted to what she did best, crying.

"Girl, you gon' mess up your makeup," Lo-Lo teased her. "Knowing how long it took me to get it perfect."

"It's okay, love," Asha pulled Shawna in her arms. "Don't listen to Lo-Lo."

"I'm just so happy," she cried into Asha's jacket. "And it don't seem real."

For any person who could personally relate, they knew that the passage from poverty to prosperity was an emotional journey. Especially when majority of the world have already counted you out.

Accustomed to Shawna's meltdowns, Noni leaned up and interrupted, "Aye, yo, it's cool if y'all wanna sit in the car and cry all night, but I'm trying to go pop champagne and see who I'm fucking on tonight. So let me out this mu'fucka."

With Asha playfully scolding Noni as they exited the car, the Butterfly Mafia marched in unison. Although her features reflected a serious expression, Lo-Lo wanted to scream from the high of excitement that coursed through her veins. As they headed to the front of the mile-long line, she loved the stares their matching jackets elicited.

With hot-pink patterns over white leather, stenciled across the chest were the woolen initials, 'B.F.M.' And adorning the back was a large image of their favorite four-winged insect, with the words 'Butterfly' above it and 'Mafia' beneath it.

Upon them entering the club, where the atmosphere pulsed with an electric energy, the female DJ lowered the music to send them a shoutout.

"I want y'all to make some noise for the Butterfly Mafia!"

Amid the collective cheers and applause as they strode to their booth, Asha acknowledged the crowd with a four-finger salute. Her braids flawless like the late Nipsey Hussle's, Noni flashed the dancing diamonds of her white-gold teeth.

"Fuck this bitch got gloves hanging out her back pocket for?" A clown commented to his female companion as the girls walked by. He was referring the baseball gloves Noni religiously carried.

"I don't know," his companion carelessly shrugged, but was secretly intrigued by Noni's natural swag.

Seated in a VIP booth, which was right next to the girls', Double-O, CJ, and their accompanying comrades rose in respect as the girls walked up.

"Wassup with the Mob?" Double-O greeted Asha with a handshake and hug.

Replying that all was well, she properly introduced him to Shawna.

As he recalled the night he'd almost taken her life, Double-O was genuinely impressed by the improvement of her appearance.

"It's good to see you," Double-O shook Shawna's hand, guessing her age to be in the late teens.

"Likewise," she replied, wondering where she knew his name from.

Inside their booth where bottles of champagne were already on ice, the girls removed their jackets to reveal Cuban link chains featuring Butterfly Mafia pendants encrusted in colorless stones. With each sizeable piece valued at $40,000, the flickering diamonds were doing the Thriller.

"It's so nice in here," Shawna leaned in to Asha, surveying the scenery from her seated position. "And how y'all get so many people in here on the first night?"

Asha's answer was simple, "Free liquor."

Along with word of mouth and posting flyers all over the city, they paid a radio station to regularly announce Skittles' grand opening. But it was actually one of the dancers who proposed the idea of free drinks. "Let them know it's twenty-five at the door, a casual dress code, and free liquor till midnight. And we'll do the rest. 'Cause once the liquor get 'em loose, they gon' wanna show out." And true enough, the dancers on all three stages were being handsomely rewarded for their provocative performances.

Noni was sipping Belaire directly from the bottle, when she caught eyes with a woman at a nearby table. Rocking tight blue jeans that threatened to burst at the seams, she was the companion of the clown who'd spoke on Noni's gloves. The clown was currently nowhere in sight, and the woman was giving Noni a look.

"Aye, y'all excuse me for a second," Noni said before exiting the booth with her bottle in hand. She approached the woman and engaged her in conversation, convinced she would sense if it was lust or larceny.

While observing her sister with a subtle smirk, Asha had a sudden thought and told Shawna to come with her. "It's somebody I want you to meet." As they walked across the room, neither paid attention to two women who sat at a table to their left. Both wearing bright-colored wigs and oversized shades, they seemed to be having fun as they took turns flinging bills at the dancers on stage.

D'Aura was behind the bar pouring a drink as Asha and Shawna walked up. "Hey, mama bear!" she beamed at Asha. "What can I get you?"

"I'm good, love. Just checking on you. Everything going alright?"

"It couldn't be better," D'Aura assured, then tapped the screen of a P.O.S. system before serving the customer their drink.

In spite of having three bartenders she deemed to be decent women, D'Aura had still taken the necessary precautions to prevent the possibility of 'over pouring'. With the help of a Bev Intel company, she had 'pourers' placed on each bottle, which cut drinks off at a certain amount. The bottles had also been weighed, which would then allow her to compare them to the number of drinks served- by way of the P.O.S. system. Grateful for being brought aboard, D'Aura intended to play her role with a business mindset.

"This our girl, Shawna that I was telling you about," Asha leaned over the bar to inform D'Aura. "A heart full of gold."

Bobbing her head, D'Aura turned to the baby face girl and held out her arms for a hug. "Any friend of Asha's is automatically a friend of mines. So whatever it might be, don't hesitate to ask."

Shawna sensed she was being truthful and accordingly replied, "The feeling is mutual."

While the three girls giggled and conversed about the club's successful opening, Lo-Lo was in the booth exchanging texts with Uno, who assured her that him and his crew were currently en route.

Lo-Lo was typing a text that warned Uno of the consequences should he fail to appear, when she happened to look up and saw Angel in the building. Having just entered the club, her intensive stare was focused squarely on Noni, who she ran down on like a defensive lineman.

But before Lo-Lo could signal for Noni to look out, Angel grabbed Noni by the arm and turned her around. "So, this why I wasn't invited? So you could be all up in some other bitch face?"

Noni snatched her arm back. "Only one person can yell at me, and it ain't you. So you better lower your muthafucking voice."

"Fuck that!" Angel barked in rebellion. " 'Cause I talked to my brother, and he said you're lying. So I want answers, Noni. And I want 'em tonight!"

As Asha and Lo-Lo were on their way over to intervene, the clown got there first. Wondering why Noni and Angel were standing over his table, he gestured with his hand for them to move around. "Take that shit somewhere else."

"Nigga, who the fuck is you talking to like that?" Noni stared him down.

"Unless you gotta twin in this bitch, I'm talking to you. This my hoe and my booth. So like I said, take that shit somewhere else."

When he made the fatal mistake of nudging Noni along, she reflexively fired off a right hand that grazed his goatee.

The clown stumbled back, touched his chin in disbelief, then pinned Noni with his most vicious look. "I'm 'bout to whoop yo' muthafucking ass!"

He went to lunge, but was suddenly blocked off by Double-O and CJ. "Nigga, watch out!" the clown fought to get around them. "That bitch put her hands on me!"

Built like weightlifters on steroids, two beefed-up security guards strutted over to identify the problem.

"She put her muthafucking paws on me!" the clown cried. "That's the muthafucking problem. Now either y'all get her ass outta here, or I can have my lil' youngins come through here and air this bitch out!"

One of the guards glanced at Asha, as he'd been secretly informed of the club's ownership. And due to the hefty wages he received for the 8-hour shift, he'd bounce the clown out on his head if Asha gave him the word.

But she wouldn't get the chance, for Noni decided to handle it herself.

"Bitch ass nigga, we can go outside and catch that fade," she challenged the clown over Lo-Lo's shoulder. "And the loser gotta leave."

The clown jerked his head toward the door in confidence, "Let's get there, then."

Over half the club followed the fighters outside. While there were some who doubted it would actually go down, there were others who were familiar with Noni's reputation. And they were excited to finally get a chance to see her in action.

As Noni unhooked her chain, Shawna worriedly turned to Asha, "You really about to let her fight him?"

"She gone end up exploding if I don't," Asha sensibly explained. "So this'll help let out a little pressure. But trust me, love, she gon' be alright."

With money exchanging hands as bets were noisily made, Noni handed Shawna her B.F.M. chain. "Here, hold my bet," she grinningly joked before putting in her mouthpiece.

Noni was slipping on her baseball gloves, when someone had the bright idea to pull their car around and use their headlights to illuminate the fight.

"This how we get down in the "D", my baby!" a man in Buffs boasted, as he went live on I.G. "And I got fifteen-hunnid on my girl, BFM Noni."

Using their phones to record the bare-knuckle brawl, the crowd came together to enclose Noni and the clown as they squared off. Noni briefly locked eyes with his female companion and winked at her.

As the two opponents circled each other, looking for an opening, Noni was also calculating time and distance. Minus the headgear and gloves, for her this was another sparring match at the gym.

Let me see where he at, Noni thought to herself, then feigned a jab to see how he'd react. When he flinched before throwing a wild overhand, Noni knew for a fact that the clown couldn't fight. Ooh I'm 'bout to show out, she smiled to herself.

With a rhythmic weaving of her head as she closed the distance, Noni lowered her guard to lure him in. He took the bait as she got within reach and swung a fundamental two-piece. She leaned left to avoid his jab, slipped right to dodge the cross, then countered with a crisp right hook.

"Ohhh!" the crowd erupted as the clown stumbled sideways.

Driven by emotion, he angrily came forward, swinging for the fences. A move she predicted, she crouched and pivoted, and was now behind him. When he whirled to face her, she fed him a three-piece special, then danced out of reach as he tried to swing back.

"Nigga, that bitch got work!" shouted someone in the crowd. "He can't even touch her!"

Fearful and frustrated, with the heckling crowd only making it worse, the clown decided to employ his advantage, strength. If he couldn't outbox her, he could surely overpower her. Bracing himself as he charged in on Noni, he ate several more punches before getting a hold of her shirt. When he took her to the twelfth and brought her back down on the hood of a car, Double-O slyly withdrew his weapon and looked at Asha for permission to squeeze.

There was a sudden scream, followed by the clown pleading for someone to intervene. "She got my dick! Somebody get her off me!"

A firm believer that rules didn't exist when it came to a street fight, Noni had turned the tables by employing her own tactics.

"Don't get mad, nigga!" Noni yelled as they were broken apart. "You grabbed me first and I grabbed you back. Now is you trying work or wrestle?"

Amid boos and insults from the boisterous crowd, the clown summoned his companion with a nudge of his head. "Come on, we outta here."

While following the footsteps of her favorite sugar daddy, the woman looked back at Noni and returned the wink. Unbeknown to the clown, she had given Noni her number minutes after they met.

As a lively Noni led the way back in Skittles, the two wig-wearing women walked to their rental. Inside the car, Mecca and Unique removed their disguises.

"I can't even lie," Unique smiled, bringing the engine to life, "I enjoyed watching her whoop that nigga ass. That lil' girl something else."

"Yeah, she is," Mecca smirked, also genuinely impressed by Noni's performance. "But no matter how likeable they might be, we can't forget what they did."

Unique wore a thoughtful expression while steering through traffic. When she slowed to a stop at a red light, she turned to her sister and voiced what she was thinking. "Have you thought about what made them kill Pee-Wee and Otha? I mean, what would make them girls do something like that themselves? And we know it wasn't no robbery."

"I already know what you're thinking, cause I've thought about it myself," Mecca replied. She was referring to the revenge they had sought and attained for their sister, Amiri. "But regardless of what their reason was, it doesn't excuse the fact that they murdered members of our family."

With this being something Unique had given serious thought, she didn't fully agree with Mecca's opinion. "We both know Pee-Wee and Otha was vicious as fuck. So let's just say, hypothetically, that they raped one of them girls. Is you saying we would still get revenge for some shit like that?"

Mecca frowned, for it was unlike Unique to question her authority. "Ni-Ni, we not 'bout to play the hypothetical game. All we know is they killed out peoples in cold blood."

"Mecca, I don't never go against nothing you say, and you know that. But I just don't see them two girls doing no shit like that in broad day, in front of hundreds of witnesses, unless it was behind some foul ass shit."

"So what you suggesting, Unique? You wanna just forget about it? You wanna forget the two people who put their lives on the line for us, on too many occasions to count?"

"You taught me that real women do real things, even when ain't nobody looking. What we did for Amiri was justified by all means. She was innocent and didn't deserve that. But this, we don't know what actually happened. It might be a reason we've missed twice. So all I'm saying is, let's just dig a little deeper and find out what really happened.

'Cause I gotta feeling there's more to the story than what we know."

This girl getting soft on me, Mecca reasoned to herself. But for the sake of their bond, she decided to comply. "Alright, we'll do it your way. But we gon' start with our old friend, D'Aura."

Upon their entering the club, Mecca and Unique had been surprised to see D'Aura working behind a bar in Detroit. A native of their hometown, she had not only attended their same high school, but had once even met their mother. So naturally these two sisters were concerned when they witnessed the connection D'Aura shared with Asha, for she could easily reveal to the girl not only their identities, but worse, the location of their mother's senior resort.

Although that scenario was unlikely to happen, Mecca had monstrous mind that believed it was best to abort an issue while still in its infancy stage.

Chapter 20

Back at club Skittles, Asha was washing her hands in the restroom, when Angel walked in. "Girl, you must got magic in them hands." She smiled while on her way to a stall.

Lost, Asha looked in her direction and asked, "What you mean by that?"

"Everything you touch turn to sugar!" Angel answered before flushing the toilet. She emerged from the stall and joined Asha at the sink. "I've met a lot of girls, my age and older, but none have come close to being on your level. And I gotta admit, it's intriguing as hell."

Despite being mildly discomforted, Asha masked it with a friendly smile, "Thank you, Angel. And you're a sharp woman yourself. 'Cause not everyone could've pulled off the role of a kingpin's wife."

Downplaying the praise with a shrug of her shoulders, Angel replied, "Yeah, but that wasn't really that hard. You gotta think, I've been around it my entire life. But you..." she moved closer to Asha, "you gotta brain that's like a capsule of brilliance. And sometimes I wonder if you really know how special you are."

Wow, she really trying to pop that corn on me, Asha smiled to herself in amusement. *No wonder Noni got caught up in her feelings.*

When Angel mistook Asha's stillness as a signal of consent, she leaned in closer and attempted to kiss her.

Asha stepped back. "Angel, you know this can't happen."

"But Noni don't want me, so why can't it?"

"Because she's my sister."

"But what if she said she didn't care, would it make a difference then?"

Considering her arrangement with Perez, along with the fact that she wasn't attracted to girls, Asha was thinking of how to proceed, when Angel grabbed her hand and earnestly pled, "Just be my safe place for one night, Asha. Let me crawl inside you and hide from the world. Please."

Asha was left speechless. For how did you respond to a statement so deep and poetic?

The restroom door suddenly opened and a drunken woman stumbled in. She took in the two girls, then pointed her finger and teased, "I see what's going on in here with you pretty girls. But don't mind me, I gotta pee like a racehorse."

Grateful for the timely intrusion, Asha withdrew her hand from Angel's and fled the scene.

Upon her return to the booth, Asha poured herself a shot of Remy and downed it in one gulp. As she refilled her glass, she could feel the heat of Shawna's inquisitive gaze.

"It's time for the main event!" The DJ announced, eliciting a room full of whistles and cheers. "And this gon' be something real special, y'all. So I hope you saved some singles."

The club was suddenly enveloped in a suspenseful darkness. Then, seconds later came the beginning lyrics of a Beyoncé classic.

"I've been drinking...I've been drinking/ I get filthy when that liquor get into me/ I've been thinking...I've been thinking/ why can't I keep my fingers off it?/ baby, I want you..."

When the lighting was restored, Lo-Lo was posing in the center of the main stage, wearing a pink overcoat and matching stilettos. She began to sensually sway to the music, lip-synching the lyrics while sharing her blue eyes with various people. When she caught sight of Uno, who attentively stood several feet from the stage. Her look made him feel like he was the only man in the room.

Undoing her coat as she continued to sway, Lo-Lo gradually unveiled her natural C-cups. With her nipples a mystery behind butterfly pasties, over her left breast was the permanent design of her B.F.M. ties. Upon fully removing the coat, she gave view to a God-given figure that infected the hearts of less fortunate women with feelings of envy.

The beat dropped at the 1:36 mark and Lo-Lo exploded into a choreographed routine. Her rhythmic movements were a well-blended mixture of ballet, gymnastics, exotic dancing, and her own creativity. Hands down, the girl had moves that belonged on screen.

Both hauling duffel bags, two of Double-O's comrades made their way to the stage. And as the club was spellbound by Lo-Lo's performance, they showered her with the money Asha retrieved from the stash house. While the club idea was in honor of Lo-Lo, it was also the method that Asha selected for the cleansing of their money. For who could contest the dollar amount a gentlemen's club generated over a weekend period.

Standing alone as she watched Lo-Lo's show, Asha thought she'd implode from her inward excitement. In life, there was no greater feeling than when a vision evolved into one's own reality.

As Lo-Lo was bringing her routine to a close, she presented the crowd with the butterfly wings tattooed on her cheeks and began making them flap. But what stole the show, was when the lights went out and she pulled down her thong to expose a tattoo on her yoni that glowed in the dark. Arranged in an arc were a number of multi-colored Skittles, and written beneath them was the well-known slogan: "Taste The Rainbow".

When Lo-Lo sashayed from the stage, leaving the crowd in a frenzy, security stood guard as Double-O and his crew collected the money from the stage in black hefty duties.

Slinging the trash bags over their shoulders, they marched to the back room where Asha awaited.

"I see somebody been withholding a lot of information," Uno smiled, as him and Lo-Lo stood by the bar. " 'Cause not only can you dance like a mu'fucka, but why you ain't tell me you the owner of this joint?"

"Who said anything about me being the owner?" Lo-Lo played dumb.

Uno just looked at her, and she bursted out laughing before admitting it was a co-owned business. "And besides, if I tell you all my secrets, you ain't gon' have nothing else to chase."

He agreed with a grin, "Facts. But don't forget my b-day coming up."

"What that gotta do with me?"

Sporting a diamond chain over his Louie Vuitton windbreaker, Uno grabbed either side of her jacket and drew her closer. "A nigga been keeping count. And we done exchanged hundreds of texts, and talked on the phone for hours, like we back in junior high. But I ain't even had a whiff of that lil' shit. So if my patience don't prove I'm different, then maybe I am chasing my mu'fucking tail."

Lo-Lo did have to admit that the man was adamant about acquiring her affection. She also couldn't deny her addiction to the emotional high that come from his relentless pursuit. The past two months had passed in a blur, as she hourly looked forward to their nightly conversations. Which was why she found herself assuring him that his efforts weren't in vain.

"I'm not the type to play games," Lo-Lo began. "But on account of everything I've seen and experienced, I know the importance of being overly cautious. Because a lot of times we meet people, give them a piece of us, then later regret it and wish we could take it back. So why be in a hurry to get hurt? And think about it, don't no man go to a dealership and pick out the car with the most mileage on it. So you should be thankful these thighs ain't seeing heavy traffic."

Truly impressed by Lo-Lo's logic, Uno was thinking of a witty reply, when his attention was seized by something nearby.

"What you looking at?" Lo-Lo nosily inquired, then turned to see Noni as she was posing for pictures.

"Your girl something else," Uno smirked, recalling certain rumors and her parking lot spectacle.

"Yeah, she is." Lo-Lo warmly smiled. "But her heart solid gold, and I love that girl much as humanly possible."

Also watching Noni was someone whose thoughts were less sentimental. Throwing back a double shot of Patron, Angel was thinking of teaching Noni a lesson about toying with her feelings.

Chapter 21

Still mildly tipsy from her alcohol consumption, Asha was in her bedroom dancing to the soulful sounds of SZA's "Ice Moon". With her eyes closed as she softly sung along, she heard her bedroom door open but didn't immediately turn to acknowledge the intruder.

Asha opened her eyes when the song ended and smiled at her twin. "We did it, love. We're officially on our way to becoming legitimately successful women."

With her hands thoughtfully wedged in her pants pockets, Noni nodded in response.

"What's wrong with my Noni?" Asha frowned in concern.

"I'm good," she shook her head. "But do you really think me going to see Angel is a good idea?"

"I do. Because it's clear she's infatuated with both of us. You physically, and me mentally. So to starve her of both could make her hateful enough to lash out in spite. So I until I figure out a solution, I just need you to pacify her."

Asha walked over to Noni and took either of her hands. "There's people who place a lot of importance on self-preservation. But me personally, I value your life over mine. Because I wouldn't be no good if you wasn't here with me. I love Shawna and Lo-Lo from the bottom of my heart. But I love you from the depth of my soul. You my little baby, and every decision I make is with you in mind. And you do trust me to always watch over you, don't you?"

"Of course," Noni answered, with tears in her eyes.

Asha could sense there was something else weighing on her sister's conscious. "What is it, Noni?"

"I just wish that..."

"You just wish that what?" Asha earnestly implored.

A set of tears rolled down her cheeks. "I just wish that I would figure out how to help Asha, and make her happy."

"But seeing you happy does make me happy."

"I'm talking about your own personal life. We're almost twenty-one, and you've never even been with a boy before. You're not into girls, so there has to be something holding you back. And I think I know what it is, and it's all my fault."

"How could you say that?" Asha squeezed Noni's arms.

"Because maybe if I wasn't the way I am, then that wouldn't have happened to me that night. And that didn't happen, then you wouldn't have whatever issue it is you can't seem to get over."

Saddened by the weight of guilt attached to her sister's conscious, Asha gripped her sister in a fierce embrace. "It's not your fault, love. So please stop thinking like that. Regina did this, not you. Her misplaced loyalty affected us both. I could never hold you responsible. And who you are as a person is you were intended to be, or you wouldn't be who you are. And as far as my personal life, that's something I'll address once I make sure everyone I love are in winning positions. And once that happens, I give you my word I'll focus more on myself."

After sending Noni off with a kiss on the cheek and instructions to be careful, Asha wiped her eyes as she ran to her sanctuary, the shower.

Inside the bathroom, Asha cut on the water and, without even removing her clothes, sat on the floor of her walk-in shower. As the hot water rained down over her, she drew her knees to her chest and convulsively cried.

It was true. Asha had never been sexually involved with a boy before. In fact, she'd never even been kissed. And it wasn't that she lacked an attraction to the opposite sex, because there had been people in the past who had caught her eye. But after witnessing the vicious assault of her twin sister, Asha's mind was marred by memories she couldn't erase. Whenever she'd imagine herself being intimate with a man, her fantasy was always invaded by vivid images of Noni's attack. It was then she would cringe at the idea of being penetrated by a man.

While this was a phobia that Asha was desperate to shed, she didn't know where to begin. And she was too ashamed and self-conscious to seek the counsel of professional help.

It was so frustrating for Asha to know that she could help everyone else, but not herself. But her deepest depression derived from the thought of being sentenced to life in a state of loneliness. Though she entertained, and allegedly accepted the likelihood of her never falling in love, she knew the absence of affection was emotionally unhealthy.

If only she could overcome her phobia and find a man who would tell her she was special and whisper poetic statements such as those similar to Angel's.

***

"Oh my god, Noni, yes!" Angel cried as she clutched a fistful of carpet. With her back deeply arched and her face on the floor, she was accepting her punishment with pure satisfaction.

When Noni had initially arrived on her doorstep, Angel attempted to act as if she was uninterested. She stated she was not some toy that Noni could play with whenever convenient. "...and right now we're not even on the level where you can just be showing up at my house unannounced. I mean what, you didn't bag nothing at the club? Out of all them bitches I watched you talked to, I'm the last resort for your little horny ass feelings?"

When Noni didn't respond, Angel grew angry. "You better answer me. Or get the hell out my house. 'Cause if you think—"

Noni grabbed her by the throat. "What the fuck I tell you 'bout that yelling shit? You up in this bitch barking like my shit ain't gangsta. Fuck wrong wit' you?"

Although she made a scene of struggling to break free, Angel was sexually ignited by the aggressive treatment. And Noni knew it. Which was why she shoved her hand inside Angel's peach colored panties.

Withdrawing a middle finger full of whipped cream, she forced Angel to suck it clean before breathing in her ear, "I'm 'bout to punish this pussy till you pass out."

As Noni was presently planted behind Angel, fulfilling her pleasurable promise, her eyes emitted a steady flow of tears. Because not only was she in tune with her twin sister's pain, but she also dealing with demons of her own.

While Asha had never been with a man, Noni had never made love to any of her partners. She always opted for hardcore sex. And though most women enjoyed the ordeal, for Noni it was actually a reenactment of her painful experience. For she was simply inflicting the pain that had been inflicted on her.

Chapter 22

Monday morning...

Having breakfast at Burger King, the Butterfly Mafia were seated in a booth at the rear of the restaurant. With her weapon resting on the seat between her and Lo-Lo, Noni had a clear view of either entrance.

"Look, Noni!" Shawna suddenly exclaimed, passing her phone across the table. "Girl, you got over three hundred thousand views!"

Global overnight, Noni had gone viral after the video of her fighting a man had been posted to social media.

As Noni got hype, Lo-Lo reproved her, "Noni, that ain't nothing to be celebrating. You did that shit at our club, on opening night. That's not the type of attention we wanna attract."

"Oh, so you don't think you attracting attention with that lil' love affair you having with that nigga, Uno?"

"And what's that supposed to mean, Noni?"

"It means, rapping ain't all them niggas into. They say half his crew hit licks. So I hope you ain't letting that nigga rock you to sleep."

"Rock me to sleep?" Lo-Lo repeated, feeling somewhat insulted. "What you don't think I could sense if he was running game? And for the record, me and him ain't did shit but some kissing."

Noni looked at Asha. "What happened to 'no distractions while run up a bag'? 'Cause the way she acting over this nigga, she definitely distracted."

Although she agreed with Noni, Asha would wait until she was alone with Lo-Lo to address the situation. "Aye, listen, we not doing this right now," she scolded them both. It ain't the time, and it damn sure ain't the place. So y'all dead that shit and hug. Right now."

Knowing Asha was dead serious, Lo-Lo and Noni unhappily obeyed.

They were finishing their breakfast sandwiches in silence, when Asha asked Noni is she intended on ordering the Terrence Crawford fight on Pay Per View the following weekend.

"I thought about it," she shrugged, still harboring an attitude. "But I don't know yet."

Shawna looked up. "Ain't that the boy from Nebraska? Noni, I thought that was your new favorite fighter?"

"It is," Lo-Lo spoke up. "She order all his other fights. But right she still mad, that's all."

"Well, I guess we won't be needing these then?" Asha said, laying four tickets on the table.

When Noni looked down and saw what they were, her eyes bulged in disbelief. "Twin!" she exclaimed, picking up a ticket to see that it was ringside. Forgetful of the firearm that laid in plain sight, she hopped up from the table and went around to hug and kiss her sister. "Thank you so much!"

As Noni's reaction attracted inquisitive stares, Lo-Lo casually placed her purse on top of Noni's pistol.

"When did you get these?" Noni asked, as she returned to her seat and continued to gawk at the tickets.

"About two weeks ago," Asha answered.

"Ohhh shit!" Noni's eyes widened upon having a sudden thought. "We going to Vegas!"

Asha nodded, "Yup. And y'all know what that mean."

"What?" Shawna was eager to know.

Grinning mischievously, Asha said, "We gotta go shopping. Spare no expense shopping."

Overflowing with joy, Noni grabbed Lo-Lo and gave her a big kiss on the cheek. "I love you, Lo-Lo."

"Y'all see this shit?" Lo-Lo laughed. "Now she got them tickets, and she wanna be hugging all up on me. Talking 'bout, 'I love you, Lo-Lo'."

As they joined in laughter, Asha's phone buzzed from a received text message. She read it and said, "Come on y'all, let's roll. Buddy ready for us."

They were leaving the restaurant, when Lo-Lo leaned into Noni and returned the kiss. "I love you back, girl."

Noni smiled in response. And just like that, all was forgiven and forgotten, as real friends did.

Minutes later, Asha wheeled the Denali into the parking lot of a PNC bank. Parking in a space near the front entrance, she pressed a button to raise the rear hatch and hopped out. Grabbing two bags from the trunk, she called for the hatch to be lowered and marched towards the bank.

Behind the SUV's tinted windows, Noni watchfully sat in the backseat with a weapon on her lap the length of an infant. Modified to a fully an automatic, her finger fondled the trigger in preparation to protect.

Inside the bank, Asha was met by the manager, Mr. Lawler, who had approved her loan. "Good morning, Ms. Kincaid. How may I help you?"

"I'd like to make a deposit."

Eyeing both bags, the manager summoned the presence of a male employee. "I need this counted," he sternly instructed before transferring the bags.

As the employee spun on his heels and hurried to a back room, Mr. Lawler led Asha to his office. "I see business is booming already," he smiled from behind his desk. "Looks like I made the right call in signing off on that loan."

"You did," Asha affirmed. "And the way things going, I'll have it paid off in no time. Speaking of which..." she withdrew a wad from her jacket and tossed it on his desk. "That's my way of expressing genuine gratitude."

Asha was fully aware of the kinship between generosity and influence. While those who took shelter in selfishness wouldn't relate to such reasoning, she firmly believed that all charitable deeds promised future rewards.

Mr. Lawler was placing her gift in his desk, when there was a knock at the door. "Come in!" he called after closing the drawer.

"Sir, I have the count," the male employee informed, holding in the air a yellow post-it. Motioning the man forward, Mr. Lawler accepted the post-it and was duly impressed by the amount written on it.

"I may be in the wrong line of work," the manager joked with Asha once the door had been closed. "One hundred fifty seven thousand dollars in one weekend is quite impressive."

Asha smiled, "You'd be surprised at the money men will spend for the sake of a visual."

With a receipt in her pocket as she climbed back in the truck, Asha squeezed the wheel and boastfully squealed, "The Mob on the move and can't nobody stop us!"

As they passed the receipt around and screamed in celebration of their victory, Noni magically produced a bottle of Bel Aire. "Who y'all know popping champagne before noon?"

Though it was reckless behavior, they all took a sip on the strength of the moment. And if Tupac was alive right now, he surely be proud; as these were four female roses that grew from the concrete.

***

When Lance entered the visiting room of the federal facility in Milan, Michigan, he beamed at the sight of his sister.

"Why didn't you tell me you was coming?" He asked while tightly embracing her. "I could've got my haircut and stuff."

" 'Cause you're my brother, not my man." Lo-Lo laughed. "So how you look is unimportant. All that matters is you're here. And I can see you."

Overjoyed by his sister's presence, he assured her he was now in much better spirits. And just when he thought he couldn't be any happier, Asha and Noni were admitted into the visiting room. Shawna was still on probation and unable to get approved.

"Noni!" Lance leaped jumped to his feet, which earned him a cautionary look from a nearby guard.

Rocking Off White outfits, the twins held the attention of every visitor in attendance as they strode toward Lance. Whereas Asha owned an air of nobility you couldn't help but inhale, Noni owned a glare that gave proof of her passion for gunpowder.

As he observed the room, Lance reveled in the way his friends were regarded. It gave him a sense of importance to be linked to such women. And they didn't let him down, as they embraced him like family; with Noni ruffling his hair as she did when he was younger.

"So what's good with my lil' bro?" Noni asked as they settled around the table. "How you holding up, my baby?"

Unable to stop cheesing, Lance said he was maintaining to the best of his ability. "I mean, I still ain't really made no friends. But you know I ain't never been good at that."

"Lil' bro, fuck these niggas!" Noni loudly stated. "I heard they gossip worse than girls anyway. And if any one of 'em offend you in any—"

"Noni, is you trying to get us kicked out already?" Asha interrupted. "Damn, girl, we just got here."

Stubborn as ever, Noni leaned forward and lowered her volume, "Like I was saying, lil' bro, don't hesitate to tell me it any one of these clowns offend you in the slightest. I don't give a fuck if it's him not putting enough mashed potatoes on your tray. Just let me know, and I'll go holler at his peoples before they clear count."

Bright eyed and grinning, Lance promised her he knew her number by heart.

As time often did when enjoyment was involved, the hours flew by. Then, to Lance's dismay, a guard announced that visiting hours were over.

Asha gave him a hug and promised to soon return. "And we gon' get you through this, lil' buddy. So keep your head up. And don't tell your sister, but I put $2,000 on your books. Tear that commissary down!"

Bobbing his head in obedience, his mind was already making a list.

As him and Noni embraced, she quietly reminded him, "Don't forget what I said, my baby. 'Cause for you, I'll make a rock bleed!"

Accepting her word as gospel, he was genuinely comforted by her supportive pledge.

"I love you so much," Lo-Lo declared, squeezing him in her arms. "And you know you can call me whenever you feel like it, right?"

At the mention of calling her, Lance remembered to deliver a message. "That dude Monster keep asking about you. And when he heard I had a visit, he wanted me to ask you if he could have your number."

She thought for a minute. "You know what, give him my email address. And tell him we'll start off with corrlinks."

Lo-Lo had no desire to date a dude in jail, but she was willing to keep it cordial for the sake of her brother.

Lance was in such good spirits that he forgot to get emotional as they exchanged goodbyes. Waving farewell before exiting the room, he would've never believed that his next visit would have a much different effect.

Chapter 23

With her daughter tugging on the hem of her jacket, D'Aura stood outside her apartment building as a group of movers were packing her possessions into a mid-size U-Haul. Her new house in Detroit was finally ready, and she was truly excited by the timely transition.

"Mama, can we go to McDonald's?" Polaris pled for the umpteenth time. The little girl didn't know how it had happened, but her mother's *yesses* now outweighed her *nos*. And she was taking full advantage.

"We'll be leaving in a minute, baby," D'Aura patiently explained. "And as soon as we do, I'll take you to McDonald's. So can you wait just a little longer, please?"

Her 5-year-old mind saw an opportunity. "Can I have a milkshake, too?"

Smiling at the friendly extortion, D'Aura agreed to meet her daughter's demands. "Yes, you can have a milkshake, too."

"Oooh... I love you, mama!" Polaris hugged her leg.

As D'Aura was thinking how fortunate she was to have met an angel named Asha, her phone rung. She answered it laughing, "Yeah, I definitely know who you are now."

"What you talking about?" Asha smiled on the other end.

"Girl, why was I literally just thinking about you, and then you call my phone. Yeah, you can act like you a human if you want to, but I'm hip to you."

Asha laughed before asking if her presence was needed. " 'Cause I can jump on the road right now."

"Nah, girl, you good. The movers almost done, so I'll be leaving here in a few."

"I still say you should've left all that stuff behind and started over. And it would've been fun helping you pick out new furniture."

"You gone get your chance to help me. But just not until we can do it on my own dime. 'Cause Lord knows you've done way more than enough for me. Shit, I was thinking I might as well let you claim me on your taxes."

"What my baby over there doing?" Asha asked in reference to Polaris. "Why she so quiet?"

"Cause she over here extorting my cool ass. When we leave here I gotta get her milkshakes and some more shit."

"Put her on."

Polaris accepted the phone in one of her chubby hands. "Hello!?"

"Hi, pretty baby?"

"Hi, Asha!" Polaris exclaimed, instantly recognizing her voice.

"How my pretty baby doing?"

"I'm fine. I'm 'bout to go to McDonald's and get a Happy Meal and a chocolate milkshake. Do you want something, too?"

"No, baby, I'm okay. You just make sure you enjoy yours."

"Okay."

"Alright, put your mama back on."

Polaris was passing the phone back to D'Aura, when she suddenly took it back and told Asha in the sweetest tone, "I love you, Asha."

As she felt her heart melt, Asha genuinely replied, "I love you, too, Polaris."

When D'Aura got back on the phone, Asha told her she had tears in her eyes.

"Yeah, I was caught off guard by that one myself. But it just goes to show that even a child can sense how good of a person you are."

They were discussing daycare arrangements, when D'Aura announced that the movers were finished and she was officially on her to becoming a resident of Detroit.

"Call me the minute you get here. And I'll meet you over there."

"Yes, mama bear," D'Aura joked before disconnecting the call.

As she strapped Polaris into her car seat, D'Aura asked, "You really like Asha, don't you?"

She nodded.

"And that's a good thing," D'Aura confirmed. "And if mommy ever gotta go to Heaven, I would want you to be a good girl for Asha. You hear me?"

Again, Polaris solemnly nodded.

"Alright, sweetie," D'Aura kissed her forehead, "let's get you to McDonald's."

As she drove off, D'Aura was oblivious of the slate-blue Buick that followed suit behind her. Inside the trailing sedan were Hotrod and Dogbite. Acting on orders from Mecca, they would wait until the opportune time and advise D'Aura to disclose whatever information she had on the twins. And in the event of rebellion, they were given the greenlight to use excessive force.

For the sake of a salary he desperately needed, Hotrod would convince her to talk, even if it meant removing fingers of a 5-year-old.

Chapter 24

As Asha led the way, the Mob marched across the tarmac at Detroit International. With each girl pulling a Louie Vuitton luggage case, they stepped in the direction of a private jet; which Asha had legally chartered will the help of her bank manager.

A female flight attendant stood at attention as the girls walked up. "You must be Ms. Kincaid," she smiled at Asha.

"I am," she confirmed, producing her ID as proof.

After a careful glance, the attendant volunteered to load their luggage onto the plane, to which Asha politely declined. "We're not here to overwork you, ma'am."

"But it's not a problem. In fact, it's part of my job description."

Asha removed a small fortune from her pocket and held it out for the woman to take. "I specifically requested a female host. These my sisters behind me, and we represent woman empowerment. So trust me, we good."

Eyeing what was surely a quarter of her yearly wages, she expressed her deepest gratitude before leading them up the plane's short flight of steps.

Upon entering the Boeing business jet, Asha was greeted by a pilot whose posture implied military experience. "It's a pleasure to meet you, Ms. Kincaid," he gripped her much smaller hand in a firm shake. A master at masking his outward emotions, the pilot was taken aback by Asha's youthful appearance. He'd been expecting someone older than his youngest daughter.

Replying that it was a pleasure to meet him as well, Asha regarded the man with a direct stare. Whether it was a veteran or a villain, she refused to be fearful of any man but God.

"Well, you can call me Pete," the pilot continued. "And if there's anything you need, don't hesitate to inform your attendant. At ONE flight, we aim to please our valued customers. So make yourselves comfortable, and there's plenty of refreshments on board."

Shawna covered her mouth at the beauty of the 12-passenger cabin. "Oh my God," she mumbled in amazement while slowly taking it all in. This was unlike anything she had ever foresaw in her future.

Noni roamed further into the plane and returned a moment later to share her discoveries with wonder filled eyes. "Yo, this mu'fucka gotta real live bedroom in it. And it ain't just one, but it's two bathrooms. Twin, why the hell would you get something bigger than our damn house? Girl, this thing like a mansion with wings!"

Chuckling at Noni's silliness, Asha and Lo-Lo recalled having similar reactions during their first experience. To step from pissy project hallways to the spacious gallery of a Gulfstream indeed gave birth to dreamlike feelings.

When Shawna and Noni got scared during takeoff and clung to each for dear life, Asha and Lo-Lo couldn't refrain from using their phones to record the hilarious image.

This what life really about, Asha thought to herself. *Making memories with the ones you love.*

Once the plane levelled off above the clouds, the flight attendant entered the cabin with a cheerful smile. "Hey ladies," she handed out small brochures, "this contains a list of our complimentary menu. So feel free to order whatever you like."

No longer deathly afraid, Noni spoke up, "Listen, love, we too geeked to eat right now. So if you could just get us a bottle of champagne and some glasses."

As the girls giggled and sipped while headed to Houston, where they would briefly stop before going to Vegas, they had City Girls bumping through the surround sound system.

Flew in on a jet I got chartered/ half-uh-million all hunnids my start-up/ everybody trapping, turning apartments to the Carter/ press a button on the whip make it start up/ I believe in God not in karma...

***

Back in Detroit, D'Aura and Polaris were lying in bed watching a kids movie, when there was a sharp knock at the front door downstairs. D'Aura initially considered it odd, being as though she was new to the neighborhood, and Asha had flown to Vegas. While thinking it was likely someone who had the wrong house and would realize their mistake and leave, whoever it was knocked again. She threw on a robe, told Polaris to keep watching the movie and that she'd be right back.

Downstairs, D'Aura peered through the peephole and took in the face of a light skin boy she didn't recognize.

"Who is it!?" she called through the door.

"It's about the twins!" Hotrod answered in an urgent tone. "Double-O in the car and we finna shoot up to the hospital. Asha got shot."

D'Aura quickly unlocked the door and snatched it open. "What—"

Hotrod rushed the door and sent her stumbling back. When she ran in the direction of the staircase, he quickly caught her and threatened with a chrome weapon, "Bitch, I'll break both yo' legs if don't be still. Now try me."

Behind them, Dogbite came in and closed the door.

Cursing herself for being so stupid and naive, D'Aura could only think about the safety of her little girl, who she prayed stayed in the room.

As if he had read her thoughts, Hotrod asked her where her daughter was.

"Please don't hurt my baby. She only five."

"Then you better answer every question I ask. 'Cause if not, her blood on your hands."

"Listen, I got some money put up in my closet. It ain't much, but y'all can have it. Please."

"Bitch, we ain't here for no fucking chump change!" Hotrod snapped. "Now you gone tell me everything you know about them twins, or I swear this house gone be a real bloody crime scene."

"Mama?" Polaris called in a small voice, standing across the room with her favorite teddy bear in hand.

"Polaris, go back upstairs, okay, sweetie?" D'Aura urged as calmly as she could. "And mama will be up there in a minute."

The little girl sensed something was wrong and didn't budge.

"Baby, please go back upstairs for me," D'Aura now tearfully pled, inwardly praying for divine intervention. She had looked around for something to grab and use for a weapon. But on account of dealing with two armed men, such a useless attempt would surely erase any chances of her daughter's survival.

Polaris surprised everybody, when she dropped her teddy bear and charged the man closest to her mother. "Leave my mama alone!" she hammered Hotrod's legs with her tiny fists.

When he roughly shoved her to the floor, D'Aura sprung like a wild cat and tried to claw out his eyes. Hotrod put her to sleep with a vicious uppercut.

As Polaris ran over to shake her mother and tell her to wake up, Hotrod told Dogbite to take the little girl swimming.

"Swimming?" he repeated in confusion.

"Nigga, she seen our face. And I'm assuming you ain't got the heart to shoot her, so take her in there and drown her lil' ass in the tub."

Polaris screamed at the top of her lungs when Dogbite grabbed her and he quickly covered her mouth with his hand. As she wiggled in his arms and tried to bite him, he carried upstairs in search of the bathroom.

While he had never taken a child's life, Dogbite had also never been in a position where a child could be the witness that got him sentenced to a life bid in prison. So he would do what was necessary and pray for repentance.

Downstairs, Hotrod was standing over D'Aura's motionless body, when a shrewd idea popped in his head. Whether D'Aura talked or not, she was dead either way. But with what he had in store, he was sure Mecca would applaud his method and maybe even give him a bonus.

"Yeah, Mecca definitely gon' love this," he demonically grinned, removing the belt from D'Aura's robe.

Chapter 25

With nearly 20,000 in attendance, the T-Mobile arena in Los Vegas was packed to its capacity. Among those in attendance were notable celebrities, athletes, and other figures of underworld prominence. This was hyped as the fight of the year, with majority in support of Terrence "Bud" Crawford, the boy from Nebraska who outboxed the odds.

As the main event was just moments away, there was a couple who sat a row behind ringside and couldn't but notice the four vacant seats in front of them. "I wonder whose seats those are?" the foreign-face woman asked her boyfriend. "I mean, who spends that kind of money and don't even show up?"

While responding that it was likely some idiot who purchased them just so no one else could, he noticed a number of heads began turning toward the isle way, like a fighter was making their appearance. But when he craned his neck, he saw what resembled four baby polar bears headed in his direction.

Marching in single file formation, the Butterfly Mafia were officially in the building. With their pupils peering through the tinted lenses of Cartier "Buffs", the girls were draped in hooded white Minks that grazed the ground. And tagging behind them were a pair of bellboys. Every nearby person stared in curiosity as they pardoned themselves while sidestepping down the row to the four vacant seats.

The inquisitive couple sat back and exchanged a look.

When the Minks were removed in a synchronized fashion, the onlooking crowd couldn't believe their eyes, for decked out in designer were four young ladies. And in addition to their BFM chains, each girl wore a second Cuban Link that featured a massive butterfly pendant that glistened with clear and pink stones. This was their reason for stopping in Houston, where they picked up the pre-ordered pieces from the famous Johnny Dang.

Handing their costly coats to the bellboys, Noni turned to take a seat and took notice of the inquisitive couple. She lifted her head at the woman in acknowledgement, to which she responded with a bashful smile and feminine wave. As her boyfriend scowled at the flirtatious exchange, Noni sat down and casually smoothed the back of her braids; showcasing a four-finger ring that spelled her name in crushed diamonds.

The arena's noise level rose to a deafening volume as Terrence Crawford made his appearance. And although her ringside seat brought her within feet of a fighter she bragged to be the best, Noni maintained her composure and observed "Bud" Crawford with a cucumber's coolness.

When the bell rung and the fight got underway, Noni was so engrossed in the action that she was unaware of Asha watching her.

It wasn't a mystery that Noni was in love with the sport of boxing, and Asha was thinking of how it was time for her sister to fully pursue her dream. Because not only did they now have the finances to fund it, but Asha would rather see her twin stacking belts than bodies. So upon their return to Detroit, she and Noni would have a serious talk.

After retaining his titles in a near flawless fashion, Terrence had exited the ring, when he surprisingly paused before Noni and proposed they take a picture.

Completely caught off guard, Noni's first reaction was to look at Asha, who grinningly encouraged her to take the picture. Regaining her senses, Noni held her phone at an upwards angle and snapped several flicks.

"I see you nice with the hands," Terrence smiled at Noni, referring to her viral video. "But don't let it go to waste. 'Cause didn't nobody believe in me when I was coming up, but now look."

If the girls weren't regarded as stars upon their arrival, the interaction with the champ had just stamped their excellence.

"How the hell you make that happen?" Noni asked Asha, as the mink-wearing women left the arena.

Asha shook her head. "I didn't."

"Come on, twin, stop playing."

"Nah, for real, it wasn't me."

"Girl, you should've seen your face when he told you to take that picture," Lo-Lo teased Noni from behind. "And why you look straight at Asha?"

" 'Cause I know she did it. And y'all know she did it, too."

As they stood outside, waiting for valet to bring their rental around, Asha confessed, "Nah, for real though, it was Shawna. That was her work, Noni."

"What?" Noni turned her wide eyes on Shawna. "Girl, you mean to tell me this whole time you had me thinking—" Noni paused at a sudden thought and started wagging her finger at Shawna accusingly, "You know what, I should've known. 'Cause you was acting way too quiet."

A grinning Shawna shrugged and sweetly replied, "I just do what I can when I can for a friend, that's all. But like Lo-Lo said, you should've seen your face, Noni. 'Cause your reaction definitely made it worth it."

It was during Shawna's stint in rehab, when she unknowingly befriended a relative of Crawford's. In spite of their six-year age difference, Shawna and the woman discovered they had something else in common besides addiction, a relation to loyalty. While on Facetime with her cousin one day, the woman had called Shawna over to say

147

hi. Upon doing so, she recognized his face as being the boxer Noni highly favored. So when Asha bought the tickets, Shawna simply asked a favor from a friend she spoke to on a regular basis.

Noni grabbed Shawna and squeezed her in affection. "Oooh, I just love your lil' chocolate ass. Got me all excited and shit."

As Shawna was basking in the warmth of Noni's embrace, the valet pulled up in their spaceship-size rental. English white over seashell and black interior, it was a Rolls Royce Phantom. Stuffing their Minks in the trunk, Shawna joined Asha up front as Lo-Lo and Noni settled into the soft rear seating.

Asha was whipping the wide body with just her left hand, when Noni suddenly laughed in the backseat. "Aye, yo, I still can't believe I actually met that nigga, Terrence."

"And you got the pictures to prove it," Lo-Lo chimed in.

"But more importantly," Asha spoke up, "Don't forget what he said about wasting your talent. 'Cause the same way you was watching the fight, best believe people will be watching you with the same fascination. And I wasn't gon' say nothing yet, but, maybe it's time for you to focus more on boxing and less on the streets."

While giving serious thought to her sister's statement, Noni had no doubt she could go pro. And like her coach once said, she'd then have the financial freedom to take care of her people, and whoever else she wanted to help. *I could really become the woman's world champ.* The thought was so intriguing that she broke out in goosebumps.

"Asha, girl, where you taking us?" Lo-Lo inquired, leaning up front and laying a loving hand on Shawna's shoulder.

"Come on now," Asha briefly glanced over her shoulder, "You know we can't come to Vegas and not do no gambling. So I brought a few dollars for us to jack off at the casino."

"Now that's what I'm talking 'bout!" Lo-Lo did a little dance. "I'm 'bout to catch that beginners luck and hit for some crazy shit. I'm talking like, over a hundred thousand dollars."

Amid their riding down the brightly lit strip of Sunset boulevard, Shawna was dreamily gazing up at the stars in the Phantom's headliner, when she said something Asha couldn't quite make out.

"Girl, what you just say over there?" she looked at Shawna with a curious grin.

Shawna turned to her and repeated, "The Stars Are Ours."

***

Courtesy of fake IDs, the girls gambled and drank at different casinos. And although Lo-Lo didn't strike gold, she learned that losing money could be so much fun.

It was currently in the wee hours of the morning, and Asha and Shawna stood before the large window of their suite that overlooked the city. They were twenty-four floors from ground level, and the view was breathtaking. Curled up on separate sofas behind them, Lo-Lo and Noni competed to see who could snore the loudest.

"Asha, I know I tell you all the time, but thank you so much for saving me," Shawna said while taking in a city that never slept. "And I don't like to think of myself as weak, but I accept me for who and how I am. Everybody not meant to lead. And I'm okay with that. Because how could a war be won if it was all generals, right?"

Asha smiled at her reasoning, which did make perfect sense. "Yeah, I guess you right when you put it like that. But it's different when it comes to us, love. 'Cause we all four equals. Regardless of whatever mistakes or bad decisions you might've made in the past, your life is just as valuable as ours. So matter who or what we up against, we always gon' stand on the front line together."

Shawna turned from the window. "Girl, you like Big Meech and Tupac wrapped up in one."

Although pleased by the compliment, Asha laughed, "Dang, girl, how you just compare me to two dudes?"

Shawna giggled, "Nah, I meant to say you the girl version of 'em. Cause you a generous leader and an advocate of the struggle at the same time. And as much as I'm content with being me, if I had to be anybody else, I would want it to be you."

Moved by the heartfelt disclosure, Asha reached for Shawna's hand. As they stood in silence, she considered telling Shawna about her phobia. But she just couldn't do it. So instead, she leaned into Shawna and together they watched the sunrise.

Chapter 26

With Shawna riding shotgun, Asha was zipping through traffic in a gray and white Slingshot. Bobbing their heads to Keyshia Cole's "Ride", both girls wore designer shades and Air Jordan hoodies.

They were flying down Joy Road, when Asha lowered the music to take an incoming call. "Hello?" she answered through the pod in her left ear.

"What up doe?" Double-O greeted on the other end.

"What's good, brodie?"

"I ain't on shit. Just left the shop from getting a line up. 'Bout to shoot to the store and play these numbers real quick."

"Okay, that's wassup," Asha said, slowing the Slingshot to a stop behind several cars at a red light.

"So, how was the fight?"

As Asha explained it was something he'd have to attend to understand, a tinted SUV pulled up on the passenger side of the Slingshot.

When Shawna angled her head in its direction, the back window lowered, giving view to Double-O. He lifted his head in acknowledgment before tossing a satchel out the window, which landed on Shawna's lap.

"One-fifteen the lucky number today," Double-O told Asha through his own air pod. He had no intention of playing the numbers, but was simply telling her the dollar amount in the bag. With money coming in like clockwork, they wisely switched up the method of their exchange each time.

After carefully scanning the area for cherries-and-berries, Asha made a U-turn and sped off in the opposite direction. Her and Shawna looked at each other and laughed, then Asha turned the music back up and they resumed singing along with Keyshia.

Along with their trap house, which was still being relocated every thirty days, Asha had appointed Double-O and CJ as sales rep' over bulk distribution. With Perez providing as much product as she was willing to purchase, it was senseless to stick to serving only small quantities. So whether it was a kilo or a gram, the Butterfly Mafia would collect every coin.

Upon returning home, they found Noni on the living room floor, playing her video game. She glanced in their direction and asked how the trip went.

"Like butter," Shawna volunteered, smiling for no apparent reason.

"Yeah, well, don't get used to that Slingshot. 'Cause I bought that for me."

Asha grabbed a pillow off the couch and threw it at Noni. "Shut your stingy butt up. That's all ours. And Shawna can drive it whenever she feel like it."

Pausing the game, Noni hopped up and threw the pillow back at Asha. "How you gon' tell her she can use it, and she don't even know how to drive?"

"Because I'm the big sister and I said so," Asha said before throwing the pillow back at her.

When Noni returned fire and ran, Asha and Shawna chased her upstairs, where Noni disappeared inside her room. Signaling for Shawna to be quiet, Asha went in her room and grabbed two pillows, one of which she gave to Shawna.

Creeping towards Noni's room, Asha put her ear to the door and could feel her twin doing the same thing on the other side. Asha looked back at Shawna, counted to three with her fingers and charged into the room.

Armed with her own feathered weapon, Noni jumped from behind the door and a pillow fight ensued.

After comical minutes of swinging and screaming, the girls were breathlessly sprawled on a floor full of feathers. "I can't believe y'all just jumped me," Noni panted.

"And I can't believe you tried to run," Asha laughed. "Like we wasn't coming for that ass."

Shawna rose up on her elbows. "Aye, where y'all know Double-O from?"

The twins instantly turned serious. "Why, wassup?" they asked in unison. Double-O was a friend, but Shawna was family. And there wasn't a man on earth they wouldn't murder on her behalf. Period.

Pleased by their protective reaction, Shawna quickly calmed their concerns, "Nah, it ain't nothing like that. But I know him from somewhere."

Explaining how they'd met him through his cousin, Teer, Asha said that Double-O and his deceased friend, King, once had a crew called "The Fam".

"King?" Shawna repeated. "Kavoni had a little brother named King."

"You know Kavoni?" Asha asked, recalling the phone conversation in Reverend Daniels office.

"Yeah, him and Puma was like brother and sister. And on the day she went missing was the last time I talked to him. He had told me to take Martha and hide, but he never showed up. And then I seen him on TV for being charged with her murder, and bunch of other stuff. But I knew he didn't kill Puma. He loved that girl more than life."

"I was on the phone with him some months ago," Asha revealed.

"When?" Shawna asked. "Oh my God, I need to talk to him. Let him know I'm okay, and see if it's anything he need me to do."

"Well, I didn't actually talk to himself, but I was in the room when Double-O did."

"So that's where I know him from," Shawna nodded, as it all made sense now. She couldn't wait to see Double-O and tell him who she was.

"So was Puma as vicious as they say she was?" Noni inquired. She'd been compared to her on more than one occasion, and wanted details from a direct source.

Shawna wordlessly got up and left the room, leaving the twins to exchange a curious look. She returned a minute later with the box she'd gotten from her grandmother's house. When she opened it to reveal a full-size Glock, they both looked at Shawna in shock. "Damn, girl, why you ain't tell us you packing up in here?"

" 'Cause it ain't mine. This was Puma's gun. She nicknamed it Martha, cause she said it be cooking shit like Martha Stewart."

Noni smiled, nodding her head. "Yeah, I like that. That's original."

"But to answer your question about Puma," Shawna picked up the gun and handed it to Noni, "you see those little nicks on the side of it?"

Noni counted six of them and shrugged, "Okay, what that mean?"

Shawna leaned forward and answered in a secretive tone, "That's how many bodies she had." As the twins lifted their eyebrows at the number of kills, Shawna added, "With just that gun alone."

Noni was regarding Martha with fascination, when Shawna told her, "I think you and Puma would've been friends. 'Cause y'all similar, but different."

"How?" Noni genuinely wanted to know.

" 'Cause it's like..." Shawna thought of how to best to describe it, "y'all both on some stud shit, but she was a little more physically delicate than you. Like, Puma didn't play, but she wasn't about to be fighting no boys and shit. Oh, and another thing, y'all both super overprotective. It's like, y'all can turn your hearts from gold to cold in the blink of an eye."

Asha happened to glance at the time. "Oh, shit! Come on y'all, we gotta hurry up and get dressed and get over to the club. Buddy having that party, remember?"

As a result of Skittles growing popularity, Asha had been receiving a number of rental requests in regard to the club being used to host various parties and events. Her only stipulation was that if exotic dancing was involved, the women would have to be the club's own employees. What Asha was doing was instilling in her dancers that Skittles was a business based on unity. Her philosophy was simple: it's hard to harm what you need the most. Meaning, if you keep them well-fed, you'll likely be the last they see as a meal.

Without fail, the twins peeked out the front curtains before leaving the house. Whether it was the feds or felons, they trusted their instincts to alert them of danger. Once almost certain there was no one lurking, the trio filed out through a side door and jumped in the Denali.

With her strap on her lap as she backed out the driveway, Noni told Shawna to cut on some music.

"Aye, hold up right quick," Asha said from the backseat. "Let me try to call this girl, D'Aura, again."

Since returning from Vegas the day before, Asha had been calling D'Aura, but to avail. While a day or two of not talking was nothing unusual, Asha was becoming concerned by D'Aura's failure to return her calls.

Once again D'Aura's phone rung until the voicemail picked up. Tired of leaving messages, Asha ended the call. As she was on the verge of telling Noni to stop by D'Aura's house, Noni spoke first, "Twin, stop worrying so much. That girl good. She in a new city where don't nobody even know her. And besides, it ain't like she involved in nothing no way. Watch we get to the club and she standing behind the bar."

Despite Noni's assurance, Asha couldn't shake the uneasy feeling in her stomach. But, going against her intuition, she sided with her sister and admitted to being paranoid, a decision she would ultimately come to regret.

Upon their arrival at the club, the first thing Asha noticed was the absence of the Nissan. Noni turned in her seat to address her sister's look of concern, "It's still early, love. If she don't show up before the night over, then we'll go over her house and get to the bottom of it. Now quit looking like our dog just died."

When they went inside, Lo-Lo was at the bar, laughing with the dancers, Ray-Ray and Kiva. As Lo-Lo rose to greet her girls, she instantly picked up on Asha's energy. "What's wrong, love?" she softly inquired.

Shaking her head, Asha acknowledged Ray-Ray and Kiva before making her way to the office in back.

Lo-Lo shot Noni a questioning look, to which Noni replied, "She ain't heard from D'Aura since we got back, and she panicking."

Lo-Lo thought for a second. "But we only been back two days."

"My point exactly," Noni emphasized.

Not feeling their exchange, Shawna excused herself and went to go join Asha. She wouldn't repeat a word of their conversation, but she'd tell her girl she was willing to tag along to D'Aura's house right now.

"I hate to run out on y'all," Lo-Lo grabbed her purse, "but I gotta go see a man about a horse."

Noni scoffed, "So you gon' learn the hard way, huh?"

"What?" Lo-Lo smiled.

"Girl, I ain't dumb. The only horse you thinking about is the one you hoping that nigga, Uno, got between his legs."

"Oooh!" Ray-Ray looked at Lo-Lo. "Why is this my first time hearing about a Uno?"

"This ain't that Bandgang nigga, is it?" Kiva asked.

"Yeah, that's him," Noni confirmed.

"Girl, be careful with that," Kiva warned. "That nigga mixed in with nothing but goons, goblins, and gangbangers. They'll be done found your white ass stuffed in a mattress like drug money."

"He ain't even like that," Lo-Lo readily defended. "We been talking for months now, and he ain't showed not one faulty sign."

"The spider can't catch the fly without a seduction," Kiva wisely counseled.

"I hear everything y'all saying," Lo-Lo said while headed toward the door. "And I appreciate the concern. But you calling the wrong hand on this one. Trust me."

As Lo-Lo left out the door, Kiva shook her head at the girl's naive nature. But she understood that sometimes heartbreak was the most effective teacher.

Wondering why Asha had yet to tell Lo-Lo to end the affair with Uno, Noni made a mental note to remind her sister of the dangers Lo-Lo's behavior was posing. But for the time being, she asked Ray-Ray to grab her a bottle of Bel Aire.

"Girl, you know D'Aura and your sister got every bottle weighed and accounted for. And I ain't about to lose this sweet ass job."

"Asha might be the oldest, but I'm the boldest," Noni said while going around the bar to fetch her bottle herself. "'Cause when shit hit the fan with that nigga, Uno, who you think gon' be the one to get on that John Wick shit."

As Noni drunk directly from the bottle, Ray-Ray and Kiva exchanged a brief look; for both women were well aware of her murderous skills.

**

Blowing a blunt of High Octane, a bare-chested Uno sat on the sofa in the living room of his high rise apartment.

THE BUTTERFLY MAFIA 2 | FUMIYA PAYNE

Today was his 25th birthday, and he was hoping to be on the verge of receiving his most anticipated present.

As someone who'd been born and bred in the belly of the beast, Uno was of the select few who turned out different. True, his posse consisted of parolees and predators, but in shark-filled waters, what else was there to swim with?

But since being forced off the porch at the tender age of twelve, Uno had never played a role in the rape of a woman, the finesse of a friend, or any other roguish racket resulting from a defective character. He took pride in standing on morals and principles, and vowed that if music paid off he'd pack up his property and put the "D" in his rearview.

Uno was exhaling a nose full of smoke, when a half-naked figure emerged from his kitchen, carrying a birthday cake. "Damn, baby," he put the blunt in an ashtray and rose to regard her from head to toe. His manhood noticeable stirred in arousal, as he thought how her thighs looked more edible than the desert in her hands.

Wearing four-inch heels and lace undergarments, Lo-Lo smiled, "Y'all see something y'all like?"

"Do we?" Uno emphatically replied. "You know how long I've been waiting to get a bite of that shit. And I ain't talking 'bout no cake."

Right after her return from Vegas, Lo-Lo had reached out to Uno in regards to the celebration of his birthday. She had warned him that nothing was promised, but that they could link up and let the evening organically unfold. Assuring her he'd be without any expectations, Uno gave Lo-Lo something of his less than a handful had, his address.

Uno noticed something odd about his cake and inquired, "Yo, why that joint ain't got no candles on it? How I'm supposed to make a wish?"

"See, that's your problem," Lo-Lo playfully scolded, "You worried about all the wrong things. Now, would you sit back down and let me do me?"

"My fault," he threw up his hands in surrender. "You got it. Don't shoot."

Lo-Lo sat the cake on a coffee table. Then, with his undivided attention, she began to sensuously sway to a melody in her mind. She swatted his hands when he attempted to touch her and continued to move in a mesmerizing manner.

Licking his lips in lustful anticipation, Uno silently pledged he would please her even if it took all night. He thought she was different on some many levels. Unlike majority of the women he met, she'd made him wait for a taste of what he knew would lead to addiction. So like any civilized man who encountered something rare, he'd take the unselfish steps to ensure that it became his.

In the midst of her dancing, Lo-Lo suddenly turned and purposely lowered her bottom on top of the cake.

"Why you do that?" he asked in confusion.

Presenting him with her cheeks that were covered in icing, Lo-Lo looked over her shoulder and blew his mind, "Because now you get to have your cake and eat it, too."

Chapter 27

As the bachelor party at club Skittles was well underway, Asha came out the back office to acknowledge the host. Having viewed him on camera, he had long dreads and appeared to be in his mid to late forties. Joined by another man, who was light complected and impeccably dressed, their table was absent of any alcohol beverages.

Asha was approaching the table, when she locked eyes with the man who sat with the host and the hairs on her neck stood up in alarm. In spite of her displaying no visible reaction, she was slightly disturbed by a man she deemed to be dangerous. And for some strange reason, she thought about Dullah.

Although the man flashed a nonthreatening smile as she reached the table, the lack of emotion in his coal-colored eyes belied his attempt to come off as harmless. Asha had no doubt that the man seated before her was a coldblooded killer.

As Asha was introducing herself to the host, Noni came over to join her in support. She had been watching her sister from her seat at the bar, and instinctively felt that her presence was needed.

Introducing himself as D.D. Porter, the host pointed to a younger man who was visibly enjoying his two-woman lap dance. "And that's my nephew right there. By this time next week, he'll be a married man. But I can't say happily."

Unsure of why he felt the disclosure was needed, Asha thanked him for his business and encouraged him to enjoy his night. As her and Noni were headed to the office, Asha looked back before going inside and saw that D.D.'s friend was stalking their every step.

Along with the conference table, the back room, which they now referred to as office, had everything from leather sofas to mini refrigerators. And mounted on the wall was a 70-inch monitor that showed sectional images of the club, both inside and out.

"Why you staring at that screen like that?" Shawna spoke, startling Asha out of her trance like state.

She masked her jumpiness with a smile, "I was just in deep thought about something. Don't mind me, love."

"You still worried about D'Aura?"

Before Asha could answer, there was a knock at the door. She quickly returned her attention to the monitor, and the killers were nowhere in sight.

"Wait!" Asha told Shawna as she reached to unlock the door.

Noni instantly looked up from her phone at the fearful tone of her sister's voice. "Twin, wassup?"

Instead of responding to Noni, Asha called out, "Who is it?"

"It's Kiva, girl. It's some man out here who say he need to talk to you."

The reactive look on Asha's face caused Noni to lift her jacket and withdraw a weapon from her waistband.

Motioning for Shawna and her sister to step back, Noni quietly unlocked the door, then shielded the gun along her leg and yelled for Kiva to come in.

Upon Kiva entering the room, she immediately felt the tension and grew discomforted. "Aye, I was just trying to let you know that some older dude was asking about you. But I can tell him y'all busy if you want me to."

"Nah, send him in," Noni urged, as the safety on her semi was disengaged.

Appearing in the doorway was the man Asha sensed to be a coldblooded killer. With his hands clasped at his back in a composed gesture, his eyes skillfully scanned the room before settling on the semi Noni partially concealed. His reaction gave no indication of the slightest concern.

"Wassup?" Noni challenged in an unfriendly tone. "Who the fuck is you?"

There was the flash of a subtle smirk before he answered in a levelled voice, "Your father."

To Be Continued...

Chapter 28

A LETTER TO LEROY

Dear Leroy,
I once wanted to literally curse you and physically hurt you... and I viewed you as the valueless image of a villain without virtue.

But as a seasoned soldier who's simply in search of much-needed closure... I'll maintain my composure and deliver with dignity this heartfelt disclosure.

What your point of planting a seed when you knew you wouldn't nurture what was certain to sprout? and why did your presents for Christmas always consist of garments of grief and toys of self-doubt?

As a child I would curl beneath my covers and wonder during many sleepless nights...like, what is so wrong with me that he doesn't even want to be a part of my life.

I would look for your presence, but you were never nowhere to be possibly found...I was in need of your essence, but in the depth of my tears you allowed me to drown.

I'll always remember I'd wait on the porch, just hoping and praying that this time you showed...but the years I suffered just made me tougher and taught me to stand on all ten of my toes.

But can you imagine the hurdles I encountered on account of your cowardly actions? or the pain I sustained in searching for someone to replace your absence?

Lock Down Publications and Ca$h Presents
Assisted Publishing Packages

BASIC PACKAGE $499 Editing Cover Design Formatting	UPGRADED PACKAGE $800 Typing Editing Cover Design Formatting
ADVANCE PACKAGE $1,200 Typing Editing Cover Design Formatting Copyright registration Proofreading Upload book to Amazon	LDP SUPREME PACKAGE $1,500 Typing Editing Cover Design Formatting Copyright registration Proofreading Set up Amazon account Upload book to Amazon Advertise on LDP, Amazon and Facebook Page

***Other services available upon request.
Additional charges may apply

Lock Down Publications
P.O. Box 944
Stockbridge, GA 30281-9998
Phone: 470 303-9761

Submission Guideline

Submit the first three chapters of your completed manuscript to ldpsubmissions@gmail.com. In the subject line add **Your Book's Title**. The manuscript must be in a Word Doc file and sent as an attachment. Document should be in Times New Roman, double spaced, and in size 12 font. Also, provide your synopsis and full contact information. If sending multiple submissions, they must each be in a separate email.

Have a story but no way to send it electronically? You can still submit to LDP/Ca$h Presents. Send in the first three chapters, written or typed, of your completed manuscript to:

LDP: Submissions Dept
P.O. Box 944
Stockbridge, GA 30281-9998

DO NOT send original manuscript. Must be a duplicate.
Provide your synopsis and a cover letter containing your full contact information.

Thanks for considering LDP and Ca$h Presents.

NEW RELEASES

BLOODLINE OF A SAVAGE **BY PRINCE A. TAUHID**

THE MURDER QUEENS 4 **BY MICHAEL GALLON**

THE BUTTERFLY MAFIA **BY FUMIYA PAYNE**

KING KILLA 2 **BY VINCENT "VITTO" HOLLOWAY**

BABY, I'M WINTERTIME COLD 3 **BY MEESHA**

THESE VICIOUS STREETS **BY PRINCE A. TAUHID**

TIL DEATH 2 **BY ARYANNA**

CITY OF SMOKE 2 **BY MOLOTTI**

STEPPERS **BY KING RIO**

THE LANE **BY KEN-KEN SPENCE**

MONEY GAME 2 **BY SMOOVE DOLLA**

THE BLACK DIAMOND CARTEL **BY SAYNOMORE**

CRIME BOSS 2 **BY PLAYA RAY**

THUG OF SPADES **BY COREY ROBINSON**

LOVE IN THE TRENCHES 2 **BY COREY ROBINSON**

TIL DEATH 3 **BY ARYANNA**

THE BIRTH OF A GANGSTER 4 **BY DELMONT PLAYER**

PRODUCT OF THE STREETS **BY DEMOND "MONEY" ANDERSON**

Coming Soon from Lock Down Publications/Ca$h Presents

BLOOD OF A BOSS VI
SHADOWS OF THE GAME II
TRAP BASTARD II
By **Askari**

LOYAL TO THE GAME IV
By **T.J. & Jelissa**

TRUE SAVAGE VIII
MIDNIGHT CARTEL IV
DOPE BOY MAGIC IV
CITY OF KINGZ III
NIGHTMARE ON SILENT AVE II
THE PLUG OF LIL MEXICO II
CLASSIC CITY II
By **Chris Green**

BLAST FOR ME III
A SAVAGE DOPEBOY III
CUTTHROAT MAFIA III
DUFFLE BAG CARTEL VII
HEARTLESS GOON VI
By **Ghost**

A HUSTLER'S DECEIT III
KILL ZONE II
BAE BELONGS TO ME III
TIL DEATH II
By **Aryanna**

KING OF THE TRAP III
By **T.J. Edwards**

GORILLAZ IN THE BAY V
3X KRAZY III
STRAIGHT BEAST MODE III
By **De'Kari**

KINGPIN KILLAZ IV
STREET KINGS III
PAID IN BLOOD III
CARTEL KILLAZ IV
DOPE GODS III
By **Hood Rich**

SINS OF A HUSTLA II
By **ASAD**

YAYO V
BRED IN THE GAME 2
By **S. Allen**

THE STREETS WILL TALK II
By **Yolanda Moore**

SON OF A DOPE FIEND III
HEAVEN GOT A GHETTO III
SKI MASK MONEY III
By **Renta**

LOYALTY AIN'T PROMISED III
By **Keith Williams**

I'M NOTHING WITHOUT HIS LOVE II
SINS OF A THUG II
TO THE THUG I LOVED BEFORE II
IN A HUSTLER I TRUST II
By **Monet Dragun**

QUIET MONEY IV
EXTENDED CLIP III
THUG LIFE IV
By **Trai'Quan**

THE STREETS MADE ME IV
By **Larry D. Wright**

IF YOU CROSS ME ONCE III
ANGEL V
By **Anthony Fields**

THE STREETS WILL NEVER CLOSE IV
By **K'ajji**

HARD AND RUTHLESS III
KILLA KOUNTY IV
By **Khufu**

MONEY GAME III
By **Smoove Dolla**

MURDA WAS THE CASE III
Elijah R. Freeman

AN UNFORESEEN LOVE IV
BABY, I'M WINTERTIME COLD III
By **Meesha**

QUEEN OF THE ZOO III
By **Black Migo**

CONFESSIONS OF A JACKBOY III
By **Nicholas Lock**

JACK BOYS VS DOPE BOYS IV
A GANGSTA'S QUR'AN V
COKE GIRLZ II
COKE BOYS II
LIFE OF A SAVAGE V
CHI'RAQ GANGSTAS V
SOSA GANG III
BRONX SAVAGES II
BODYMORE KINGPINS II
By **Romell Tukes**

KING KILLA II
By **Vincent "Vitto" Holloway**

BETRAYAL OF A THUG III
By **Fre$h**

THE MURDER QUEENS III
By **Michael Gallon**

THE BIRTH OF A GANGSTER III
By **Delmont Player**

TREAL LOVE II
By **Le'Monica Jackson**

FOR THE LOVE OF BLOOD III
By **Jamel Mitchell**

RAN OFF ON DA PLUG II
By **Paper Boi Rari**

HOOD CONSIGLIERE III
By **Keese**

PRETTY GIRLS DO NASTY THINGS II
By **Nicole Goosby**

PROTÉGÉ OF A LEGEND III
LOVE IN THE TRENCHES II
By **Corey Robinson**

IT'S JUST ME AND YOU II
By **Ah'Million**

FOREVER GANGSTA III
By **Adrian Dulan**

GORILLAZ IN THE TRENCHES II
By **SayNoMore**

THE COCAINE PRINCESS VIII
By **King Rio**

CRIME BOSS II
By **Playa Ray**

LOYALTY IS EVERYTHING III
By **Molotti**

HERE TODAY GONE TOMORROW II
By **Fly Rock**

REAL G'S MOVE IN SILENCE II
By **Von Diesel**

GRIMEY WAYS IV
By **Ray Vinci**

Available Now

RESTRAINING ORDER I & II
By **CA$H & Coffee**

LOVE KNOWS NO BOUNDARIES I II & III
By **Coffee**

RAISED AS A GOON I, II, III & IV
BRED BY THE SLUMS I, II, III
BLAST FOR ME I & II
ROTTEN TO THE CORE I II III
A BRONX TALE I, II, III
DUFFLE BAG CARTEL I II III IV V VI
HEARTLESS GOON I II III IV V
A SAVAGE DOPEBOY I II
DRUG LORDS I II III
CUTTHROAT MAFIA I II
KING OF THE TRENCHES
By **Ghost**

LAY IT DOWN I & II
LAST OF A DYING BREED I II
BLOOD STAINS OF A SHOTTA I & II III
By **Jamaica**

LOYAL TO THE GAME I II III
LIFE OF SIN I, II III
By **TJ & Jelissa**

IF LOVING HIM IS WRONG…I & II
LOVE ME EVEN WHEN IT HURTS I II III
By **Jelissa**

BLOODY COMMAS I & II
SKI MASK CARTEL I, II & III
KING OF NEW YORK I II, III IV V
RISE TO POWER I II III
COKE KINGS I II III IV V
BORN HEARTLESS I II III IV
KING OF THE TRAP I II
By **T.J. Edwards**

WHEN THE STREETS CLAP BACK I & II III
THE HEART OF A SAVAGE I II III IV
MONEY MAFIA I II
LOYAL TO THE SOIL I II III
By **Jibril Williams**

A DISTINGUISHED THUG STOLE MY HEART I II &
III
LOVE SHOULDN'T HURT I II III IV
RENEGADE BOYS I II III IV
PAID IN KARMA I II III
SAVAGE STORMS I II III
AN UNFORESEEN LOVE I II III
BABY, I'M WINTERTIME COLD I II
By **Meesha**

A GANGSTER'S CODE I &, II III
A GANGSTER'S SYN I II III
THE SAVAGE LIFE I II III
CHAINED TO THE STREETS I II III
BLOOD ON THE MONEY I II III
A GANGSTA'S PAIN I II III
By **J-Blunt**

PUSH IT TO THE LIMIT
By **Bre' Hayes**

BLOOD OF A BOSS I, II, III, IV, V
SHADOWS OF THE GAME
TRAP BASTARD
By **Askari**

THE STREETS BLEED MURDER I, II & III
THE HEART OF A GANGSTA I II& III
By **Jerry Jackson**

CUM FOR ME I II III IV V VI VII VIII
An **LDP Erotica Collaboration**

BRIDE OF A HUSTLA I II & II
THE FETTI GIRLS I, II& III
CORRUPTED BY A GANGSTA I, II III, IV
BLINDED BY HIS LOVE
THE PRICE YOU PAY FOR LOVE I, II ,III
DOPE GIRL MAGIC I II III
By **Destiny Skai**

WHEN A GOOD GIRL GOES BAD
By **Adrienne**

A GANGSTER'S REVENGE I II III & IV
THE BOSS MAN'S DAUGHTERS I II III IV V
A SAVAGE LOVE I & II
BAE BELONGS TO ME I II
A HUSTLER'S DECEIT I, II, III
WHAT BAD BITCHES DO I, II, III
SOUL OF A MONSTER I II III
KILL ZONE
A DOPE BOY'S QUEEN I II III
TIL DEATH
By **Aryanna**

THE COST OF LOYALTY I II III
By Kweli

A KINGPIN'S AMBITION
A KINGPIN'S AMBITION **II**
I MURDER FOR THE DOUGH
By **Ambitious**

TRUE SAVAGE I II III IV V VI VII
DOPE BOY MAGIC I, II, III
MIDNIGHT CARTEL I II III
CITY OF KINGZ I II
NIGHTMARE ON SILENT AVE
THE PLUG OF LIL MEXICO II
CLASSIC CITY
By **Chris Green**

A DOPEBOY'S PRAYER
By **Eddie "Wolf" Lee**

THE KING CARTEL I, II & III
By **Frank Gresham**

THESE NIGGAS AIN'T LOYAL I, II & III
By **Nikki Tee**

GANGSTA SHYT I II &III
By **CATO**

THE ULTIMATE BETRAYAL
By **Phoenix**

BOSS'N UP I, II & III
By **Royal Nicole**

I LOVE YOU TO DEATH
By **Destiny J**

I RIDE FOR MY HITTA
I STILL RIDE FOR MY HITTA
By **Misty Holt**

LOVE & CHASIN' PAPER
By **Qay Crockett**

TO DIE IN VAIN
SINS OF A HUSTLA
By **ASAD**

BROOKLYN HUSTLAZ
By **Boogsy Morina**

BROOKLYN ON LOCK I & II
By **Sonovia**

GANGSTA CITY
By **Teddy Duke**

A DRUG KING AND HIS DIAMOND I & II III
A DOPEMAN'S RICHES
HER MAN, MINE'S TOO I, II
CASH MONEY HO'S
THE WIFEY I USED TO BE I II
PRETTY GIRLS DO NASTY THINGS
By Nicole Goosby

LIPSTICK KILLAH I, II, III
CRIME OF PASSION I II & III
FRIEND OR FOE I II III
By **Mimi**

TRAPHOUSE KING I II & III
KINGPIN KILLAZ I II III
STREET KINGS I II
PAID IN BLOOD I II
CARTEL KILLAZ I II III
DOPE GODS I II
By **Hood Rich**

STEADY MOBBN' I, II, III
THE STREETS STAINED MY SOUL I II III
By **Marcellus Allen**

WHO SHOT YA I, II, III
SON OF A DOPE FIEND I II
HEAVEN GOT A GHETTO I II
SKI MASK MONEY I II
By **Renta**

GORILLAZ IN THE BAY I II III IV
TEARS OF A GANGSTA I II
3X KRAZY I II
STRAIGHT BEAST MODE I II
By **DE'KARI**

TRIGGADALE I II III
MURDA WAS THE CASE I II
By **Elijah R. Freeman**

THE STREETS ARE CALLING
By **Duquie Wilson**

SLAUGHTER GANG I II III
RUTHLESS HEART I II III
By **Willie Slaughter**

GOD BLESS THE TRAPPERS I, II, III
THESE SCANDALOUS STREETS I, II, III
FEAR MY GANGSTA I, II, III IV, V
THESE STREETS DON'T LOVE NOBODY I, II
BURY ME A G I, II, III, IV, V
A GANGSTA'S EMPIRE I, II, III, IV
THE DOPEMAN'S BODYGAURD I II
THE REALEST KILLAZ I II III
THE LAST OF THE OGS I II III
By **Tranay Adams**

MARRIED TO A BOSS I II III
By **Destiny Skai & Chris Green**

KINGZ OF THE GAME I II III IV V VI VII
CRIME BOSS
By **Playa Ray**

FUK SHYT
By **Blakk Diamond**

DON'T F#CK WITH MY HEART I II
By **Linnea**

ADDICTED TO THE DRAMA I II III
IN THE ARM OF HIS BOSS II
By **Jamila**

YAYO I II III IV
A SHOOTER'S AMBITION I II
BRED IN THE GAME
By **S. Allen**

LOYALTY AIN'T PROMISED I II
By **Keith Williams**

TRAP GOD I II III
RICH $AVAGE I II III
MONEY IN THE GRAVE I II III
By **Martell Troublesome Bolden**

FOREVER GANGSTA I II
GLOCKS ON SATIN SHEETS I II
By **Adrian Dulan**

TOE TAGZ I II III IV
LEVELS TO THIS SHYT I II
IT'S JUST ME AND YOU
By **Ah'Million**

KINGPIN DREAMS I II III
RAN OFF ON DA PLUG
By **Paper Boi Rari**

CONFESSIONS OF A GANGSTA I II III IV
CONFESSIONS OF A JACKBOY I II
By **Nicholas Lock**

I'M NOTHING WITHOUT HIS LOVE
SINS OF A THUG
TO THE THUG I LOVED BEFORE
A GANGSTA SAVED XMAS
IN A HUSTLER I TRUST
By **Monet Dragun**

QUIET MONEY I II III
THUG LIFE I II III
EXTENDED CLIP I II
A GANGSTA'S PARADISE
By **Trai'Quan**

CAUGHT UP IN THE LIFE I II III
THE STREETS NEVER LET GO I II III
By **Robert Baptiste**

NEW TO THE GAME I II III
MONEY, MURDER & MEMORIES I II III
By **Malik D. Rice**

CREAM I II III
THE STREETS WILL TALK
By **Yolanda Moore**

LIFE OF A SAVAGE I II III IV
A GANGSTA'S QUR'AN I II III IV
MURDA SEASON I II III
GANGLAND CARTEL I II III
CHI'RAQ GANGSTAS I II III IV
KILLERS ON ELM STREET I II III
JACK BOYZ N DA BRONX I II III
A DOPEBOY'S DREAM I II III
JACK BOYS VS DOPE BOYS I II III
COKE GIRLZ
COKE BOYS
SOSA GANG I II
BRONX SAVAGES
BODYMORE KINGPINS
By **Romell Tukes**

THE STREETS MADE ME I II III
By **Larry D. Wright**

CONCRETE KILLA I II III
VICIOUS LOYALTY I II III
By **Kingpen**

THE ULTIMATE SACRIFICE I, II, III, IV, V, VI
KHADIFI
IF YOU CROSS ME ONCE I II
ANGEL I II III IV
IN THE BLINK OF AN EYE
By **Anthony Fields**

THE LIFE OF A HOOD STAR
By **Ca$h & Rashia Wilson**

THE STREETS WILL NEVER CLOSE I II III
By **K'ajji**

NIGHTMARES OF A HUSTLA I II III
By **King Dream**

HARD AND RUTHLESS I II
MOB TOWN 251
THE BILLIONAIRE BENTLEYS I II III
REAL G'S MOVE IN SILENCE
By **Von Diesel**

GHOST MOB
By **Stilloan Robinson**

MOB TIES I II III IV V VI
SOUL OF A HUSTLER, HEART OF A KILLER I II
GORILLAZ IN THE TRENCHES
By **SayNoMore**

BODYMORE MURDERLAND I II III
THE BIRTH OF A GANGSTER I II
By **Delmont Player**

FOR THE LOVE OF A BOSS
By **C. D. Blue**

KILLA KOUNTY I II III IV
By Khufu

MOBBED UP I II III IV
THE BRICK MAN I II III IV V
THE COCAINE PRINCESS I II III IV V VI VII
By **King Rio**

MONEY GAME I II
By **Smoove Dolla**

A GANGSTA'S KARMA I II III
By **FLAME**

KING OF THE TRENCHES I II III
By **GHOST & TRANAY ADAMS**

QUEEN OF THE ZOO I II
By **Black Migo**

GRIMEY WAYS I II III
By **Ray Vinci**

XMAS WITH AN ATL SHOOTER
By **Ca$h & Destiny Skai**

KING KILLA
By **Vincent "Vitto" Holloway**

BETRAYAL OF A THUG I II
By **Fre$h**

THE MURDER QUEENS I II
By **Michael Gallon**

TREAL LOVE
By **Le'Monica Jackson**

FOR THE LOVE OF BLOOD I II
By **Jamel Mitchell**

HOOD CONSIGLIERE I II
By **Keese**

PROTÉGÉ OF A LEGEND I II
LOVE IN THE TRENCHES
By **Corey Robinson**

BORN IN THE GRAVE I II III
By **Self Made Tay**

MOAN IN MY MOUTH
By **XTASY**

TORN BETWEEN A GANGSTER AND A
GENTLEMAN
By **J-BLUNT & Miss Kim**

LOYALTY IS EVERYTHING I II
By **Molotti**

HERE TODAY GONE TOMORROW
By **Fly Rock**

PILLOW PRINCESS
By **S. Hawkins**

SANCTIFIED AND HORNY
by **XTASY**

THE PLUG OF LIL MEXICO 2
by **CHRIS GREEN**

THE BLACK DIAMOND CARTEL
by **SAYNOMORE**

THE BIRTH OF A GANGSTER 3
by **DELMONT PLAYER**

BOOKS BY LDP'S CEO, CA$H

TRUST IN NO MAN
TRUST IN NO MAN 2
TRUST IN NO MAN 3
BONDED BY BLOOD
SHORTY GOT A THUG
THUGS CRY
THUGS CRY 2
THUGS CRY 3
TRUST NO BITCH
TRUST NO BITCH 2
TRUST NO BITCH 3
TIL MY CASKET DROPS
RESTRAINING ORDER
RESTRAINING ORDER 2
IN LOVE WITH A CONVICT
LIFE OF A HOOD STAR
XMAS WITH AN ATL SHOOTER